THE MEMORY KEEPERS

ELEVEN FEARLESS WOMEN VOICE THEIR UNTOLD STORIES

Back The Way We Came

Michael Terence
Publishing

To every woman who yearns to tell her story
— it's never too late

There is no greater agony than bearing an untold story inside you
— Maya Angelou

Stories are medicine. They have such power; they do not require
that we do, be, act anything – we need only listen
— Clarissa Pinkola Estés

Women writers carry with them the voices of the invisible
— Yuko Tsushima

Contents

Foreword
by Rowena Chiu

I am delighted to have been asked to endorse this anthology of women's memoirs. In the wake of the #MeToo movement, it has become more important than ever to create a platform for women's voices. The female experience is often alternative, creative and diverse, but, above all, powerful. Written by women who have battled and overcome adversity, these stories are a testament to the courage and resilience of the feminine spirit and the human heart. I hope you will feel as buoyed and inspired in reading them as I did.

Rowena Chiu
Harvey Weinstein Survivor
#MeToo Activist & Advocate

Beneath the Grey Façade
poem by Micki Findlay

dust off the shadows beneath the grey façade
venture in through crusted corridors
treasure is unearthed for the one who cares to listen
she yearns for her story to be told

take the young girl's hand as she leads you through the forest
away from angry voices, embracing leafy limbs
gentle, wind-puffed kisses caress her hidden bruises
exposed by the moonlight, revealing secret sins

listen to her song, composed by fluid fingers
polished ebon notes on weathered-wrinkled parchment
an unfinished symphony swelling to crescendos
echoing the rhythms within her ageless heart

watch her performance, commanding centre stage
making love to her audience with tear-stained smiles
bathing in the limelight, she wraps the crowd in stardust
a million tiny goosebumps, frozen in time

honour the survivor who ceased to be a victim
of toxic, broken beings – angry puppeteers
rising from the ashes of shame to self-respect
her voice no longer muted, her soul not chained in fear

breathe in the fragrance within her wilted petals
silver leaves shimmer as she dances in the sun
look a little closer, beneath the grey façade

perhaps you'll see her beauty and mine, for we are one

Bear No Malice
by Lindsay Tunstall

Why in God's name am I here? Good question. Is it my subversive, damaged, bleeding heart leading me astray again? My renegade mind? The vagabond in me escaping from my life, avoiding my culture, renouncing electricity, running water, and, most importantly, my family? Lou Lou in *la-la land* fuelling my consciousness with potent West African brain food. Bob Marley, everyone calls it. Bob and I hang out often, leading to an overdose of introspection and, ultimately, more avoidance.

I keep convincing myself I live in paradise – but this is far from paradise. Poverty and disease, extrajudicial killings and torture are everyday happenings. The truth is I am lying to myself. Even the bloody termites are a nightmare and impossible to eliminate; I hear them eating my wooden bed frame at night, I know they are munching their way through the mud bricks – a voracious, seething red army. I knock on a prominent bulge in the wall, and out they pour like rice from a sack. I bring a few of my favourite chickens inside for a protein snack.

But despite the challenges, there is much I love about my life here: the vibrant colours and designs of the clothes people wear (no one dresses in grey or black, not even to funerals), the smell of *benechin* (a traditional one-pot stew cooking on a wood fire), the luxuriant face of nature, the colossal trees, the abundant wildlife, and the laughter and music of people who don't overthink as we do in the West.

Early morning is bliss, the air so much cooler in the dry season. When locals complain it's freezing, I laugh.

"You don't know what cold is; where I'm from, cold is like being inside a fridge."

I wear a hoodie and build a fire to sit by at six am; by ten, it's a sweltering thirty degrees. As a rosy dawn peeps and creeps like a shy child onto my veranda, I make an appalling instant coffee, grim for someone who likes a strong espresso, kind of tolerable when loaded with pungent mangrove honey. I wander down to the bay, passing under the flaming red blossoms of the mango trees, promises of sweetness to come. The sun laces through the palm fronds, and points of light glitter and dance on the river like a mirage.

I sit on the beach with the less-than-satisfying coffee, alone except for four pelicans majestically cruising on the water. I look up, craning my neck to watch a kettle of vultures, scenting death from high above me, as they fruitlessly circle the hospital. Hordes of scuttling crabs wave their one gigantic blue claw as if to scare me off. Monkeys cautiously make their way to the mangroves from the bush, on permanent alert for their enemy – packs of feral dogs scavenging the beach. Monkey and dog are not friends. My Dad and I were like monkey and dog. I was the monkey, and we were often not friends. I reflect on my life this morning, little knowing it would be his death by evening.

After breakfast I cross the river by ferry, from Barra village to the capital, Banjul. Usually, I prefer the local pirogues, not entirely trusting the dodgy old ferries, which Dad would have called second-hand rust buckets, if they go down, you're all going down. The chaotic stampede to disembark at Banjul starts in earnest – push, jostle, mind your feet, be careful of your bag, watch out for the enormous rumbling trucks belching black exhaust in your face – when my phone rings.

'Mum, your dad died this morning.'

Can I move back in time and not have heard those words? Rewind rewind. Is this a universal response when we hear someone close to us has gone? I stumble out of the terminal through the mass of heaving bodies, moving like a zombie, stunned as if tasered by bad news. I find a quiet place on the beach and slump on an upturned fishing boat emblazoned with the words, *Allah's Time Is The Best.* I struggle to gather the fragmented pieces of myself. Logic tells me he was ninety-four; he'd had a stroke a few months ago, but I'd never thought about him checking out permanently, it's impossible. My challenging flawed Dad is my Dad; he can't die. Would I need to explain to everyone why I looked so crushed? Of course, I didn't. I wore my face like a mask. I held it in, as you do.

By the time he was twenty-six, Dad had spent five years in some of the most notorious German prisoner-of-war camps. He held the record for the longest time spent in solitary confinement – the Cooler King of Colditz – punishment for several courageous but failed escapes. He was obsessed with the desire to fight the war from the "inside," making a bloody nuisance of himself, he called it. He was court-martialled five times for stunts that drove his captors into frenzies of irritation. Sometimes he infuriated his senior officers, who didn't take kindly to having Red Cross parcels confiscated. They were his best and worst years, but he was never the same again, never quite right.

As with the suffering and damage experienced by soldiers in the First World War, no one considered the savage effects on the human psyche of flying nightly bomber raids, being shot at and shot down, let alone the trauma of captivity. "Stiff upper lip, old chap" and all that. To most people, Dad was a war hero, a riveting storyteller, but they didn't experience his frequent drink-fuelled violence. They didn't hear him wake up screaming from another harrowing nightmare. They didn't have to navigate his unpredictable and erratic emotions.

When I had just turned twenty, Dad left Uganda, where he had worked with the Police Air Wing – mostly patrolling for poachers – another fugitive from the terror and horror that was Idi Amin and went to live in apartheid South Africa. On one of his rare visits back to London, we went for lunch in Chinatown, just the two of us. The food was delicious, the conversation less appetising. He did what so many people living in an oppressive regime do; he defended it.

'You're so naive and gullible sometimes, Lou Lou,' he said with his usual dose of condescension.

I was thirty-five with four children, for God's sake.

'You need to come and see for yourself, ducky. Before we civilised them, they were savages, killing each other with spears!'

Shit! Did I just hear that? I'd been on the demos against the racist regime where he'd chosen to live.

My scathing reply bristled with all the indignant, chilly moral superiority I could muster.

'People eyeballing each other, engaged in hand-to-hand combat, is seriously less savage than dropping fucking great bombs and indiscriminately killing countless people.'

I don't know what I expected – I hadn't thought that far ahead – it didn't go down well. He stormed out, later telling the family I'd called him a war criminal.

I could have pretended to agree with him. I could have chosen to keep the peace. I could have chosen love. Instead, I decided to be a bitch and get him where it would hurt, driving an ever deeper wedge between us. The one thing I didn't want – or did I?

Growing up with him certainly hadn't been easy; easy didn't come into it. He'd routinely batter poor Mum, and despite living in married quarters, no one ever intervened or questioned her black eyes. When he ripped her dress from her shoulder and marched her at gunpoint from an Air Force ball for some imagined slight, no one came to her aid. What on earth was he even doing with a gun there? A war relic he wasn't supposed to have?

He was terrifying, half man half beast; I'd hold my little sister in my bed, cuddling her under the blankets, desperate to keep her quiet while listening to Mum's screams. If he heard us crying, he'd burst into the room waving his belt and threatening to beat us too.

Mum finally got the courage to leave when I was five; my sister was just three. It was the evening of the Christmas play at school. I was to be Mary. She hustled us into a taxi despite my protestations that my all-important role was imminent.

'They know', she said. 'Someone else will be Mary.'

Dad stood at the front door, watching us go.

'What about Dad?' I asked.

'He'll come later.'

I knew it was a lie. I looked out of the back window as the car moved off. He stood immobile, tears pouring down his face. I waved.

I saw the headlines in the papers – *War Hero Divorces*. Divorce was not that common in 1954; it gave me a sense of shame, as though we had collectively failed as a family. We'd see him every other weekend and half the holidays. His displays of misery when we had to go, crying, holding us as if he couldn't bear us to leave, made us feel sorry for him. Holidays with him were often exciting – camping, canoeing, sailing – but always at a price. We remained constantly alert, senses tingling in expectation of another outburst of chilling violence, followed by endless tears of remorse.

His ego, severely bruised by Mum leaving, inspired him to plot his revenge with military precision. The first line of action was to marry a spinsterish woman in line for a lucrative inheritance, grateful for a husband. She jumped when he called and followed orders like a junior officer. Mum, too, had a new man; my sister and I loved him. Ted was calm and kind and made her happy, even giggly, and sometimes he'd stay overnight, leaving early the following day for work.

We must, in all innocence, have told Dad because he swiftly initiated *Operation Surveillance*. On nights when it was cloudy or moonless, he'd drive for over two hours, park his car and walk through the slumbering village into the driveway, careful to avoid crunching stones underfoot and alerting the dogs. Sneaking around the back of the large main house and with a good view of the iron staircase up to our flat, he'd conceal himself in the bushes and wait. I guess it gave him the same thrill he'd experienced in the war, creeping, hiding, fooling the enemy; in this war, Mum was the enemy. Camera at the ready, he wasn't disappointed. Dad snapped several pictures of Ted hurrying down the stairs at five am for his early shift as an air traffic controller. He showed them to us.

'I wanted to jump out and knock him down,' he bellowed. 'How dare the bastard be there all night with my kids in the flat. What kind of bad example is your immoral mother showing you? Let's see how she explains this in court.'

Cue *Operation Kidnap*. One afternoon, as we leave school, we see his VW van and run over.

'I was in the area; come on,' he says, 'I'll take you home.'

Unsuspecting, we clamber in, but instead of the short drive home, he keeps going. My sister chats away, but I feel uneasy and apprehensive. By the time we get as far as London, I finally dare to speak.

'Dad, what's happening?'

'You're coming to live with me,' he says matter-of-factly.

I'm petrified now, and my heart thumps wildly like a trapped animal in a snare.

'But Dad, we've got no clothes, no toothbrush!' I stammer.

'Don't worry; we'll get everything you need tomorrow.'

My mouth feels dry as dust.

'But Dad, Mum will wonder where we are. We should have been home ages ago!'

But, but, but… I scream silently. My head is going to combust – I'm going to be sick.

'No problem', he says, 'I'll call her as soon as we see a phone box.'

Indifferent to her pain, he gloated. 'I've told her I've got you, and I'm taking you to live with me.'

I could imagine her initial gasp of disbelief, followed by distraught sobbing. Mission accomplished.

It felt suffocating, like drowning, when Dad severed us from our life: our security, our school, our friends, the familiar scent of Mum's Elizabeth Arden Blue Grass, the calm, the routines of freedom. During the custody process, no one asked us what we wanted, as if it were nothing to do with us. We were invisible.

On the day of the ruling, Dad went in, leaving us to wait with our colluding stepmother – I later heard she'd previously stood in court and told them she'd love us as if we were her own children. Yes, thanks but no thanks, I didn't choose you to be my mum. I wanted to bolt as he came running towards us, fist in the air, triumph written all over his face.

'We won! We won!' he crowed.

We? Really? The sensation of my heart hitting my feet was palpable. It was a sentence with no hope of early release.

So it began. We spent occasional weekends and half the holidays with our disturbed mother, so broken by the cruelty and finality of the decision, her already delicate mental health shattered. She withdrew from us as if feeling too much would only give her more pain. She transferred her affection to Ted, whom she later married. We didn't mind; we wanted her to be happy. We never told her how scared we were by Dad's rages. We never told anyone.

When Dad was in a good mood, he was loving and warm, but you never knew what would trigger an outburst – a hangover, a whisky too many, some consequence of his now obvious PTSD. I trod warily, watching every word, but often got it wrong. I remember when he chased me through the house, grabbed me, and held me off the floor by my throat, his eyes crazed, I was sure he would kill me as I felt a warm gush of urine run down my legs.

I remember him pouncing from behind his study door, sending me flying across the room. I hit my head on the leg of his desk. I lay there while he kicked me hard.

'Sex before marriage is off limits! If I ever find out...' he roared. He'd noticed my newly budding thirteen-year-old breasts.

I say my private goodbye to him later that warm velvet night down by the murmuring river, the Milky Way a blazing ribbon of sparkling light overhead.

I look up to the vast night sky and remember my first flight with him when I was eight, in a rickety biplane with an open cockpit, wind blasting in my face, him turning from the controls with an encouraging smile and a thumbs up.

I remember how much I loved our Sunday morning ritual of war stories, the suspense, the daring, real-life *Boy's Own* adventures.

I think about how his bravery and determination helped make me who I am.

I think about never seeing him again.

Tears of grief and forgiveness flow down, washing away the resentment, the hurt, and the regret. I start to understand how the survival emotions of my past have shaped my life choices.

That night I dream I phone him. I say, 'Please come and see me.'

'I can't, ducky,' he replies gently, 'I've got to go.'

Fly away Dad.

As I set him free, I also begin the journey to free myself.

Forgotten
poem by Suzi Bamblett

My dad doesn't know me.

He smiles politely.

Greets me with his telephone voice.

Thinks he's staying in a hotel.

Complains his room is not that grand.

Dad doesn't understand

why his glasses don't work.

Stumbles and stutters through his eye test.

It's not the optics,

but the names of letters he can't recall.

I've no knack for Scrabble.

No truck with anagrams

or the Times crossword.

Never seen the point of long words

when short will do.

But I value

my capacity for crafting words.

One day I might lose my marbles,

like Dad and Tootles.

The words

may

      dry

         up.

Jail Tales – The Aromatherapy Saga
by Peta Heskell

Fannin County Jail, Blue Ridge, GA – September 2012

I'm escaping from jail today because I can afford $300 for private dentistry. Most of my fellow inmates have to suffer through a bad tooth with one ibuprofen at bedtime. Maybe it's my lucky day…

'Wait there.' Miss Jackson points to a bench in the corridor opposite the open door of the admin office where Sgt Carol is shuffling papers at her desk.

Jackson waddles off, her ample form straining the seams of the tight, grey shirt and male-cut trousers. The lingering fog of her cloying, cheap-smelling perfume continues to assault my senses. Here it comes – the all-too-familiar coiling up of my gut as I spit venom under my breath, 'F*tcowbitch!'

Losing everything – my freedom, my man, my dogs and my home of four years, alongside the looming inevitability of deportation – is bad enough but the petty rules and those jailers who enforce them so zealously, ignite my feral instincts.

Sgt Carol gets up from behind her desk and peeks out of the door, scanning left and right before walking over to me.

'Here, take this. Don't say anything,' she whispers, handing me a small plastic baggie containing a cotton wool ball and a tiny yellow Post-it note.

Rapid scan for any sign of the enemy before I open it… A fragrant aroma of essential oils hits me, dissolving my anger and the remnants of Miss Jackson's scent into a moment of sensual joy. Yay! I've hit pay dirt. I seal it up and slip it into the breast pocket of my *oranges*.

As the deputy sheriff leads me through the dentist's busy waiting room to the surgery, I walk tall, head up, refusing to feel less-than; last time I was here I was not wearing an orange two-piece and matching steel bracelets. After removing the cuffs he leaves me in the surgery, alone. For a few freedom-soaked minutes I relax in the comfy patient chair, staring through a large window overlooking the Ocoee River. Is it locked? Maybe I could get out, scramble down the bank, and swim along the river. I could lay low, get Sara to pick me up and drive me to Florida. I could… The opening door jolts me out of my wistful movie.

Back at the jail, Miss Jackson is waiting for me outside Sgt Carol's office. Before leaving the dentist, I'd slipped the baggie into the heel of my sock because rumour has it that sometimes they don't check socks. Pocket probed. Body felt up. Holding my breath…

'Shoes and socks off.'

Oh shit! I kick off the fake orange crocs and hand her my socks. Please don't let me lose this treasure so soon after receiving it.

'And what's this?' Jackson says, holding up the baggie between the finger and thumb of one latex-gloved hand, my socks in the other. She might as well have punched me in the gut.

'Um— '

'*I* gave it to her.' Carol is standing wide-stride at her door, one hand on the frame, the other on her hip.

My show-no-reaction face masks the rainbow arcing inside me – Miss Jackson's a jailer; Sergeant Carol outranks her. Jackson's eyes narrow, her jaw tightens – sayonara, smug smile.

'Fine,' she says, shoving the baggie at me. 'Let's go. Move it.'

She marches me back to the *pod* in silence. This time, I don't shudder at the door slamming, no hissed insults about her size. Winners don't need to bitch, and today, I'm a winner. As I inhale a hit of joy-juice, the aroma swamps my senses. Aaaah! Bliss! Her note: "Guess which oils are in this blend – it's called *Serenity*."

Wow. She's engaging with me. Another sniff – lavender for sure, maybe some neroli. Whatever, it's perfectly named. How blessed am I. Not only do I get to experience this awesome scent-fest, but someone in authority has broken the rules to gift me. And she's helped me get one over on Miss Jackson – triple bubble.

If this were a movie, I'd soundtrack it with Leonard Cohen's *Hallelujah* from *The Watchmen* – a story of fallen superheroes who rise to glory again.

How satisfying to re-play Carol verbally slicing Miss Jackson, "*I gave it to her.*" Did she secretly enjoy that? If she's into essential oils, maybe she finds Jackson's perfume as offensive as I do? Whatever, she's bent the rules to do me a kindness.

Sergeant Carol isn't involved in the day-to-day management of us inmates, but in her admin role, she's responsible for reviewing and censoring outgoing mail. I'd written to my man whining about the stink of cheap perfume, asking him to soak his next letter with cedarwood oil because it's strong and long lasting. That must be how she knew. Carol is a welcome exception, a kindred spirit, a rose flourishing in the doo-doo.

The following Sunday, I am first in line outside the pod clutching two Twinkie cakes; a bonus (some might say bribe) for spending an hour with one of four visiting pastors at *church* in the library. The door buzzes open and I step in. What's this on the floor? A white envelope with my name on it in bold, block capitals. Safely back in my cell, I open the envelope – another baggie, another Post-it note and another essential oil-drenched ball of cotton wool. It's a new blend – *Calm*. She's listed the ingredients and signed it "Enjoy, Carol." Omigod, I've got a personal aromatherapy angel.

Carol's regular Sunday envelopes are gifts that keep on giving. The aromas remain potent, safely sealed inside the baggies. I dab the cotton wool everywhere – under my nose, on my wrists, on my oranges and in the pages of my Bible. And, I share it. Sitting with some of the girls around the steel table, in our informal before-bed prayer meeting, I wave the cotton wool in the air.

'This is distilled from God-given plants like lavender and roses. Smells great, doesn't it? Here, pass it round. You can rub it on a special page in your Bible so that every time you open it, you'll be double-blessed.'

They each take turns dabbing a page; their faces lighting up as they breathe it in.

Two more days pass before the tannoy shatters my *calm serenity* – 'Heskell to the front.' Sergeant Christopher, a portly older man, with neat grey hair and sparkly blue eyes, is waiting at the pod door.

'Sorry, but there's been a complaint about some smelly perfume you have. Apparently, it's giving someone bad headaches so I'm afraid I'm going to have to ask you to bring it out to me.'

Sorry? Apparently? Afraid? Bring it out? Hmm… He's not tossing my cell and he hasn't a clue how much I have so I bring back a tiny portion of my stash.

'Is this all of it?'

'Yes, sir,' I pull a suitably humble face. 'It's very strong.'

He's one of the good guys and I don't like lying to him, but this is a game of survival. In jail, we lie as we did when we were naughty children, to escape the wrath of authority figures. We lie because small victories like hiding contraband or outsmarting a jailer or an inmate bully give us a sense of empowerment in a system designed to dehumanise us. Cue Joan Baez singing "*We shall overcome*".

This afternoon a new girl arrives in the pod. Since all the cells are full, she gets one of the extra bunks stacked against a wall in the main pod, right under the TV – it's a dud location.

"We're lucky to have cells," Loretta had told me. "In Polk County you're in one big dorm of bunks."

The thought of the jarring echoes and utter lack of personal space in a crowded room makes me cringe. New Girl appears oblivious – collapsed in a stupor.

The Voice is on TV tonight and my nemesis, Heather (signature phrase – "I'm gonna stomp your face in") has pumped up the volume to the max. She and her cronies are screeching like punters at a cockfight. After four years of basking in the natural harmony of the forest, loud noise has the same effect on me as fingernails scraping down a blackboard. Consumed by an uncontrollable rage, I rush down the stairs, cross the room, climb up on the bunk above the new girl and turn the volume down.

Heather stands up jabbing a finger in my direction. 'Fucking turn that back up!' she yells.

'No!' I stand my ground.

I want to raise my fist and chant the line from that American folk song *We Shall Not Be Moved*, but I don't; I'm not that reckless. Heather's pushing her way towards me when the new girl's voice wafts up from the bunk below.

'We don't want your Cadillac ways here…'

For an instant it goes quiet. Her hilarious turn of phrase defuses my anger. I know when I'm beaten. I slip off the bunk with a muttered "whatever" and slink back to my cell.

Heather's got the TV on full blast again and my makeshift earplugs – balled-up strips of material from an old pair of knickers – are useless against the din. I can't focus on reading so I pull the thin grey and blue checked blanket over my head and sob.

In jail, crying and country music, even in the Deep South, are a no-no. They have a way of stirring up emotions – heartache, despair, pain – all the feelings we have to keep in check if we want to stay strong and sane. My cellmate's watching TV with Heather. No one to hear me. No one to tell me to "shut it", so I let go.

The racket outside echoes relentlessly until the TV goes off eleven o'clock. If only Heather had an off switch. No way she's going to let this go.

Cadillac Girl doesn't get up for breakfast at six. While we partake of ersatz coffee and rubbery, lukewarm, white toast spread with margarine and jam, she's still sprawled on her bunk – eyes half-open, her shaggy, short blonde hair in disarray. She looks to be in her thirties – thirty years my junior – like most of the girls in here. I figure it's time to make peace with her before I acquire another adversary; Heather is enemy enough for anyone.

After breakfast, I go back to my cell and tear off a bit of precious cotton wool. Approaching the new girl's bunk as I might a skittish animal, I raise my hands in a playful gesture of surrender and smile.

'I come in peace.'

Before she can say anything, I put a hand on my heart.

'I'm a writer and I have to tell you that line you used last night, "Cadillac ways", is so cool I wanna steal it.'

Good, she's smiling. I kneel and waft the cotton wool closer to her nose but not too close – don't want to invade her space.

'Here, take it, smell it; keep it; it'll help you feel better. It's called Serenity.'

A cautious smile as she reaches out her hand. One inhale and I can tell the aroma is working its miracle.

'I'm real sorry 'bout what I said last night. I was plum out of it.' Her melodious Southern drawl is kind of soothing.

'No worries, I get it. I'm just glad you're OK. I'm Sunny, what's your name?'

She grins and props herself up on one elbow.

'Hey, Sunny, we got the same name. They call me Sunshine.' The synchronicity doesn't escape me.

'What's up with you?' I ask, emboldened by our new connection.

'They raided the house I use for business. I couldn't get rid of the *8-balls* (an eighth of an ounce of crystal meth) but I swallowed the last two *Oxys.*'

No wonder she zoned out.

'I'm looking at two years in Blairsville…' My heart feels the weight of her resigned despair. It's the beginning of a special bond between Sunny, given name Peta, and Sunshine, given name Julie.

Later that day, sitting around the table playing Spades with Angel – a coke dealer who boasts connections to a Colombian cartel – and a couple of other girls, I tell them about my chat with Sunshine.

'Everyone loves Sunshine,' Marcie says. 'She's my dealer's dealer. Never shorts no one, not like some of 'em, and she even gives credit.' In Fannin County's drug dealer circles, Sunshine is, apparently, a legend – I've befriended a local folk hero.

Although I've only known Sunshine a few days, I've gotten some insight into her nature. She's been kind to many, sharing food and putting money on the commissary accounts of other inmates. What a stark contrast to Heather, who squirrels away underwear and food to bribe newbies in the hope of cajoling them into her clique and scoring some of their stash when they get out. In jail, cliques form easily and everyday items such as food and underwear are currency. Heather's a pro – always on the prowl, always hustling. Sunshine's generosity feels more like the real deal. Sitting next to her at lunch, I mention it.

'I'm curious; I can't help noticing how generous you are, even to strangers.'

'Nah,' she waves it away. 'I've got it and they ain't. Easy come, easy go.'

Heather's watching us, her long, thin nose scrunched up and mouth all tight. When I get up to go for a pee, I sneak a peek and, there she is, sidling up to Sunshine.

'That Heather sure don't like you,' Sunshine tells me when I get back.

'She hates me,' I blurt out. 'First day she came in, I turned her down when she asked to share my cell. She wanted me to be her "jail momma". Then she borrowed *soups* and didn't pay me back when she got money on her books, so I had it out with her. She was all "What me? Fuck off!" When I called her a fucking hustler, she went ballistic and threatened me. "I'm gonna stomp on your face and throw you over the fucking balcony." I don't think she liked it when I told her to "be my guest". She ran into her cell and started screaming and kicking the wall.'

I take a breath. I needed to vent, to express myself to a real person instead of the rants I scribble every day on lined paper, with my wobbly, four-inch biro refill. Regular biros are forbidden – they have weapon potential.

Sunshine laughs. 'Oh Lordy, she was all up in it about you - "So how come y'all hanging with that stuck-up English bitch?" Her mimic of Heather's harsh twangy voice makes me giggle. 'Shoulda seen her face when I told her I liked you. She sure weren't happy 'bout that.'

I want to hug her. Sunshine, the rock star of the pod, likes me and has stood up for me against Heather. But although I've acquired a seemingly powerful ally, Heather's animosity towards me permeates the pod like a gloomy mist. She has to be the one who complained about the aromatherapy because she's been mouthing off ever since I got it – "That fucking stink is giving me a headache." Heather has a lot of headaches. She uses them to hustle coffee. "I need coffee; it's the only thing that stops my headaches," she whines to anyone who has a stash.

Angel confirms my suspicions. 'Yep. It's her. She got her raggy old bunkie and yours to sign a grievance.'

This is not over yet; Heather's livid because she knows I've still got the oils. It doesn't help that my new bunkie, who presented herself to me as a "quiet bookworm", has been won over to the dark side with a tatty, greying bra and a Kit-Kat. The only upside is the more time she spends in Heather's cell, the less she's in my face.

Miss Jackson's voice blares across the tannoy.

'Will whoever has that stinky scent bring it out now or there'll be a shakedown.'

Oh shit! The classic manipulation – threatening to punish everyone for the so-called wrongdoing of one. My gut scrunches as I conjure up the dire consequences. They'll find our contraband – extra blankets and uniforms, empty plastic bottles, chemical cleaner hidden in old shampoo containers, sleep masks repurposed from socks and knicker elastic, razor blades, and maybe even the hooch hidden under the dustbin liner. And, it will all be my fault. There's no wriggle room – it's give it up or become a social pariah... But, before I can speak, Marcie shouts out.

'It's me miss; it's in mah Bible.'

One by one, all the girls I'd shared it with, including Sunshine, are calling out, "It's in mah Bible too." This is the Bible Belt; there is no way they are going to confiscate anyone's sacred book. My spirit phoenixes, fizzing with joy – I'm having my own Spartacus moment.

A decade after my deportation, memories and mementoes of those three months in Fannin County jail remain with me. A heart-strewn farewell note from Angel is tucked inside my Bible; the now ratty cotton wool balls are pressed between the pages although the aromas are long gone. I still have the bracelet Sunshine braided for me from Kool-Aid-dyed torn-up t-shirt strips. And, what a heartening surprise when Carol contacted me on Facebook and I got to tell her how much her gifts meant to my sanity.

Time and physical distance have shifted my perceptions.

The hostility I once felt towards Heather *"I got pregnant the first time I had sex at fifteen"* evaporated the moment she was let out. She did what she had to in the face of poverty, minimal education and a medical system that hooked her on opioid painkillers. When prescription options run out and there's no help to detox, dealing becomes the only way to support an expensive addiction.

Miss Jackson is no longer "the enemy". It can't be fun, spending all day in the same drab, sad surroundings as the inmates. Who dreams of being a jailer when they "grow up"? Like many unqualified locals, she's trapped in a system where a job in jail is one of the few legal alternatives to being a carer, working at the Dollar Store or slogging in the stench of ammonia and poop at the local chicken plant. Not a lot of career opportunities in rural McCaysville, Georgia, where one quarter of the inhabitants live below poverty level – average annual income: $23,000 and top of the crime stats: domestic abuse and property crimes.

I've tried and failed to track down Sunshine. I wonder if she ever reunited with her children, born while still in her teens and taken into care not long after. I feel so deeply for this woman whose sunny nature transcended a litany of horrors – abused from the age of four by a stepfather, raped by him at eleven, pimped out by her mother... If I were in her shoes, I'd be resorting to Oxycodone, or worse, to numb the pain. She's got a colossal mountain to climb... I hope she's found a foothold.

Up on the Downs with Diana
by Carol Prior

I'm walking slightly ahead of you but keep glancing back to check you're still following me. You're standing in the middle of the wide road, and I'm relieved there's no traffic in this quiet residential part of Bristol.

'Come on love,' I say as brightly as I can without betraying the encroaching panic that lies just below the surface of this otherwise normal summer's afternoon.

'Let's go up on the Downs. Look, we just have to cross this road...'

I tail off as I see cars speeding in both directions on the main road ahead of the road we are now walking on, an insurmountable barrier between one world and the next. I can't fully absorb this new reality where I am in charge of you, me the responsible adult, and you, a wayward child. You have always been the mother figure in our relationship, mother that you are – three times over – and motherless me, or might as well have been.

This role reversal sits uneasily between us as we negotiate that most prosaic of daily tasks, crossing a busy road, and we've crossed so many together in the last twenty years. Diana, you are in my care now, and I am scared. I'm already having second thoughts, but it's too late to turn back, so I renew my efforts to galvanise you into following me. Standing on the kerb, I look both ways and make a quick dash for it – every woman for herself – because I know it's pointless to pressurise you, and hope you follow my example, praying the cars will slow down if you're trailing too far behind me. By some miracle, we make it safely over to the other side of the road.

This is a part of Bristol Downs that I am unfamiliar with, and I can't risk getting lost with you, Diana. That would be unthinkable. Except the unthinkable has already happened. The woman I fell in love with all those years ago is now just a memory, leaving an imposter in her place.

From where we're standing, there are at least two different paths to take with no obvious landmarks to act as a guide. My sense of direction, or lack of it, has always been the source of so much frustration to me, and in six decades, it shows no sign of improvement. I must be patient with you, with myself, and with the situation. The irony is that in any other circumstance, you would have been the one to take control and we would have set out purposefully, me happy to follow you, just like Bridie used to when we took her for walks. From time to time, you ask me where we are, and it's clear you think you are still in Wales.

'Why are we here? I need to get back to feed the animals.'

'We're in Bristol Di. Remember? I went to Uni here.'

We had come on a visit in the early days of our relationship to take a trip down the memory lane of my student days. Strolling along the grandiose Georgian Royal York Crescent where I had lived on the top floor of number four with my architect boyfriend, we gazed out in wonder at the panoramic view of Hotwells basin and the distant docks. We'd had such a lovely time, but I don't mention it as I want to keep the conversation in the present, and I don't want to add to your confusion. Being in Bristol again is bittersweet, and I feel like running away. I spot a bench not too far away and decide it's better if we just sit down. What we really could do with is a café, and then we would both have something to focus on, but the only sign is for Bristol Zoo. So instead, we just sit silently side by side, the weight of unspoken words lying heavily between us.

You, who always had so many words, who spoke not in sentences, like other people, but in paragraphs about all the things you were passionate about – the environment, politics, ending the abuse of children, equality for women, and refugee rights. You who read T.S. Eliot's The Waste Land on holiday in Greece while I was devouring detective novels. You who worried about the water table and ecocide as I painted my toenails, trying not to smudge them. You, who now sit quietly beside me like a submissive child.

I loved living in this city, with its quieter pace of life and its gorgeous Georgian architecture, fresh from London in the mid-seventies, starting a whole new life as a drama student at Bristol University. I'd had two auditions at The Bristol Old Vic Theatre School, which is somewhere nearby. In a previous life, I would have reminded you of this and suggested we go and find it and revisit my old haunts. Maybe walk up steep Park St with its restaurants and bookshops. Find the Drama Department – where I'd spent three years of my life – passing by the impressive edifice of the Wills Memorial building where I took my final exams in 1976. Or… you'd have other ideas.

"Come on, let's drive to Clifton Suspension Bridge," and off we'd go and walk across it, admiring the view and marvelling at its construction. Then we'd have parked up somewhere and found a lovely little café, and I'd have reminisced some more over a pot of Earl Grey tea for two and slices of delicious homemade cake.

I'm starting to feel cold, and you're not responding to my pathetic attempts to engage you in conversation as you stare ahead, seeing nothing, so we walk back the way we came. It can't even be a hundred yards to the main road, and then in no time we'll be back at the Home, but it feels like a hundred miles. As if you're reading my thoughts, you ask me where we're going.

'We're going back to where you live Di.'

'Where are we?' You shout, wild-eyed.

'Let's go back and have a cup of tea.'

I am trying not to sound panicked, as if this is something we do every day. You're not buying it. You sense my unease and walk away from me, stating that you need to get back to your house in Wales. I catch up with you, and we are back at the main road. This time it's easier to get across because now you are a woman on a mission. I follow you helplessly as we turn down the road where the Home is.

'I'm not going back there,' you say. 'Come on, let's get the car. I can drive us to Wales. I've got to get back for Bridie and the horses…'

'You don't live in Wales, Di, you live here now, in Bristol.'

'No, no,' you say. 'Where's my car?'

'There is no car, Di.'

I hate to tell her this, but I have to get her back before she's too distressed.

'We'll take the train then,' you say, just like that, as if it's a foregone conclusion.

And for a minute I'm almost convinced we can do it. I see us as accomplices, making a break for freedom, putting two fingers up to the system. I will save you from this fate. You will not be locked away. But it's no use. Who am I kidding? We wouldn't last two minutes.

Precipitous Spirit
by Stephanie Peart

That day the sky was heavy, blanket grey. They sat side-by-side on the second of two benches. Beneath them, the water slapped, the gaps between the planks wide enough to peer through. The woman stood and moved towards the iron barrier edging the pier. The man followed, gently resting his hand on her shoulder, she turned to him, her face drawn in despair. He returned her gaze with a numb expression. They looked across the estuary but the view to the opposite shore was clouded with thick mist.

The suitcase has remained unopened through many house moves. Knowing it is there has often gnawed at my conscience. I need to open it. Heaving the case from underneath a pile of bulky household items in this large airing cupboard, I settle myself on the floor. My eyes linger on a pair of long gold velvet curtains from the tall windows in the old house. The old house.

A narrow curving staircase led up to our attic… you were six when our family moved there. Your attic room was open to the landing and staircase, quite draughty and not very private, just a door you could shut at the base of that staircase. You chose that space under the eaves with its little sash window overlooking the street – an ivory tower, candy pink clouds floating on the wallpaper which you were so fond of and which we papered together. Your elder and younger sister both had more privacy, but you didn't seem to mind. This was the place where you harboured dreams – pony riding, drama, guitar. You were a cheerful child with a myriad of enthusiasms which you followed with passion. Going to university to study literature and drama was the pinnacle of your achievement.

I unzip the case and lift the flap with apprehension. It is family-sized, made of brocade, too heavy for me to lift, the one we took to Greece. I seem to sense an aura surrounding me as I sit on the floor beside it. An odour from the fabric has imbued everything with a faint chemical smell. At first glance, I see a pile of opened airmail letters. I notice the postmarks and stamps, Greece, New York – two places where you au paired. The suitcase is brimming with other envelopes; your name, Katy, Kate or Katie, on every one. You had so many pen friends from your travels. Seeing these spread before me is almost too much to bear. Beneath the letters are Kodak photo folders, yellow and red, bank statements, student documents, rosettes from pony club days. One bundle is bound separately – the letters with Greek stamps.

You were sixteen when we took our first holiday to the island of Kos. It was 1986. Your style was eye-catching – a la Madonna, a la Toyah, tumbling amber hair tucked under a jaunty peak cap, cropped broderie anglaise cotton top, midriff showing. Greek boys flocked to try out their English but you wanted to practise your Greek… they were like bees to a honeypot.

"Mum, Dad, there's a discotheque in the village tonight, can I go?"

We didn't have the heart to stop you. I have an image of blue flashing lights, you, dancing, surrounded by youths, having the time of your life. You became enamoured with the country and returned to work there the following summer.

Gently sifting through these things, I realise what a full life you led in your twenty-two years. I sit back and muse, recalling the titles of two poems you wrote and recorded, *Amorous Sky* and *Falling Spirit*. I hope I find the tapes and hear your voice. The wealth of memories encased here comforts me, affirming my beautiful daughter lived and breathed. A mixture of pleasure and pain wash over me that you are not here.

You confided in me that you were having therapy due to your worry about second-year exams. I reminded you there was plenty more time to finish your degree and urged you to take time out and come home. On my last visit to your flat, I remember putting my arms around you in a protective embrace as I left. Your last words still ring in my ears…

"I am okay mum, coping with my anxiety – look, here are some self-help sheets from Student Health and I have that appointment with the psychotherapist next week. It'll be fine. I have my flatmate here this weekend and I have a riding lesson on Sunday. You mustn't worry."

My mission to bring you home had failed. I drove home alone.

There are two big cardboard boxes pushed to the back of this large cupboard. I drag out the first one. Inside, I find a stack of vinyl records, including your heavy metal collection. Once, so addicted to that music, you sneaked from the house to visit a club in town, your Goth style serving to disguise your age – you were fifteen. Here are cassette tapes fitted neatly in my old sewing basket. Your musical passion was such, you were often first to hear the latest hits. The last time your elder sister saw you, the latest CD album of the rock band R.E.M. was top of your list. You gave her a cassette tape with recordings of the songs… some of those lyrics could have lodged in your mind … *"when you're sure you've had enough… hold on"*. We can only guess at the truth.

I am frightened to open the second box. It has been so long. The brown gummed paper tape that once sealed it has perished. It crackles as I touch and puffs of gluey dust sprinkle my fingers. The cardboard flaps open easily to reveal yellowing newspapers neatly stacked. I hold my breath. This day had to come. I almost panic… *you don't have to do this now… you could leave it to another day…* Yorkshire Post, Yorkshire Evening Post, Huddersfield Examiner, Hull Daily Mail. I pull out the nearest. The headline hits me – MISSING STUDENT – my heart misses a beat as I see your face. It's a photo from your student card. You were always so photogenic, born with a halo of curled amber hair, but now liking it blonde. I am surprised at how calm I begin to feel. I take out another newspaper – the Hull one. It reports how you were seen in that city, sitting on a bench near the pier and questioned late at night. The policeman opened his passenger door asking why you were out so late alone. You explained that you were a Huddersfield University student and had missed the last train back. A policewoman would have been able to interview you in the police car. Satisfied, he drove off. Very soon, a Missing Person photo came on his dashboard – it was you. He went back – you had vanished.

After many hours poring over the newspapers, my initial fears melted away. Sifting through this evidence of your life a deep sadness engulfs me. It is time to let go of these things. I try to imagine what you would say to me – still holding on to them after all these years.

May Day 1993 was gloriously sunny. We were parents strolling by the river, secure in our minds that all was well. Remembering, now, the tranquillity of that afternoon, valley and dale, how we'd strayed into the grounds of that village church. I'd photographed daffodils beneath a great yew tree – dark and light next to an ornately carved headstone. My roll of monochrome film in the camera was just about used up and I was eager to see them printed. Some would be of you, having recently posed for that photo shoot next to the Henry Moore sculpture in town.

Our return home later that day is vivid in my mind. Events began to spiral out of control. Sitting here with these things, I hear my landline telephone ringing downstairs which is starkly reminding me of the call we received – it was your flatmate Helen.

The words had shot back and forth in panicky, staccato voices, the telephone so inadequate for such a crisis. How futile the frantic conversations that followed turned out to be. Jumbled disbelief that you could disappear fogged my brain. Life ground to a halt as shock waves washed over us. Three agonising weeks passed searching for you in Huddersfield, Leeds and – Hull. Another line from an R.E.M song repeated in my mind "... *take comfort in your friends..."* It was prophetic.

I wonder who was on my landline just now. Back then, it rang constantly – family, friends – all desperate for news. The Missing Person's Bureau, the Police, the University (concerned about its duty of care), and the Press (clamouring for a story). We only had one telephone in the house.

Your postcard came from Kingston-on-Hull with one line that told us you were safe – so brief. My heart lifted. You are sixty miles away. We are driving there... the car radio is playing a song which has become so familiar. Everybody Hurts burns into my brain, then, a news bulletin... a body... has been found... my heart jolts... ignore it... nothing to do with our search. How could it be? The press is waiting for us, a routine to be gone through, surely, we will do the appeal and just carry on! I push away an unthinkable thought. But when we arrive, only a police inspector walks out to greet us, his hand stretched out, concern on his face. We are ushered into a room.

My bones are stiff now. I need to stretch and stand. Forcing myself away from the boxes I make my way downstairs to listen to the answering machine. It was just a harmless message. I absently flick the switch on the kettle to make tea. I am back in Hull police station. Endless cups of tea – a posse of police officers with us – their words echoing crazily around the room as they spoke of a discovery half a mile away across the estuary. The horror of that afternoon floods back.

My ears roared... a female body... on the shore. Inside my head, I am screaming – it is not going to be you!

'Do you recognise this wristwatch?' the policewoman asked.

I froze. No words. This is not happening to our family. The wristwatch lay in a transparent bag. It was waterlogged. Clothing and socks, all inside forensic pouches... yes... no... I can't be sure, we can't... numb with shock, I forced myself to look closely at the watch. I could see it had stopped at six o'clock. My brain reminded me to breathe as I folded my arms tightly around my waist. My fingers absently claw at my wool cardigan. A hand squeezed mine. My body felt nothing. All fell away. I was floating high above – disembodied. No howling, no sobbing... that was to come. The radio announcement – the policeman's expression – the welcome cups of tea – reality began to set in as the question assaulted me...

'... the wristwatch?'...
The question hung in the air like a guillotine about to fall.

Above all, I wanted to say "no"... but I couldn't...
I managed to whisper, "yes."

It was your body that had been found on the opposite shore of the estuary – you had drowned. Nothing mattered anymore. Time stopped. The tragedy played out with you as its tragic heroine. It was in shock that we, your parents, stood on the pier where you were last seen alive. The water churned

Melancholy, I go back upstairs and return to the half-emptied suitcase with your earthly possessions spread around me. I feel great relief I faced this task, put off for so long. Unlocking your treasure trove has given me a fresh sense of what you achieved in your short life, a tangible reminder of the past, things we shared, as a mother and daughter, and as a family. I will take time to read your writing and poems and find a beautiful memory box for precious mementoes.

I have found your wristwatch still inside that polythene pouch. I unseal it with difficulty and hold it. Gold, tarnished rim around the face, hands showing the time, the black frayed strap hardened with age, damaged by water in those twenty-one days attached to your wrist.

My daughter, I still grieve that I was not able to see your body.

You will forever be remembered for your smiling countenance, your gaiety, kindness and generosity of spirit – a precipitous spirit. For your June funeral, you wore a white muslin shroud and a garland of spring flowers around your head – just as you might have worn on your wedding day. Over a hundred mourners came to remember you. We read lines from your favourite play.

Our revels now are ended. These our actors,
As I foretold you, were all spirits and
Are melted into air, into thin air…
We are such stuff
As dreams are made on, and our little life
Is rounded with a sleep.

From The Tempest by William Shakespeare.

Epilogue

That roll of black and white film… it had been tucked away, almost forgotten. I made the joyful find some years after Katy's death. Learning to develop the negatives in the privacy of the darkroom was very healing and I found solace there. I watched with pleasure as the image of her face emerged slowly from the liquid bath. Ten beautiful photographs brought my daughter to life.

Irene and the Boots
by Sarah Lionheart

Hyperhidrosis is my superpower. When I'm warm, my feet and hands drip. To hell with what the rest of the choir think, I have to take off my boots. This required hard tugging, but eventually, my poor feet were planted on the floor, creating wet prints.

Those boots were my first real attempt at treating myself. They cost me nearly £200. (The most I'd ever spent on footwear previously was £70, and those trainers are still a guilty secret.) The boots are a deep rich brown, half calf length, nice round toes, cosy sheepskin-lined, with two rather snazzy buckles on the outsides. Despite the hyperhidrosis, I get ice-cold feet. My long-suffering husband calls them my heat-seeking missiles. They locate the warm places on his back, between his thighs, and worse. He asks that I warm one foot at a time. Mostly I respect this request, but sometimes, I plead for leniency. Bless him, he surrenders.

As I sat in the shop, wanting the boots yet resigned to walking away from them, I imagined my Irene whispering to me, "Sarah, your feet could reverse global warming! You can't freeze the planet single-handedly, so buy the damn boots. You're meant to look after yourself, sweetie. That includes your feet."

This is how Irene melted my defences. A determined drip, drip of kindness. I can feel isolated but I find it hard to lower those defences against people. Irene just drip-drip-dripped away at them. Slowly and steadily, with no specific agenda, she kept being a good friend, a kind person and, darn it, loving and caring about me. At first, I didn't even realise it was happening.

She'd arrived unexpectedly one day, breezing into my yoga class, and we soon started sitting together for coffee during class breaks, catching up with the news and sharing stories. Some weeks later, she told me she'd had breast cancer, was in recovery and had been given ten years. Every year was a blessing. She'd heard that yoga helped.

About five per cent of my students appear because they have cancer and they're trying to improve their well-being. During the previous four years, three of them had died; so I held Irene's information discreetly but didn't let it weigh too heavily.

Then she joined my meditation class and came with me to the Tibetan Buddhist Monastery in Scotland. She met my other students, including Linda. I invited them both to come with me on my yearly trip to India. These trips were normally austere. I'd stay in the Tibetan Buddhist refugee settlement in Delhi with its open sewers and narrow earth paths between buildings which were literal rat runs. After being bitten by mosquitoes and devouring moist *momos*, I'd catch the overnight bus or train up to the Himalayan mountains, live simply for a few weeks in a monastery guest house attending teachings, and return to Delhi for a few days before flying home.

Irene broke the pattern. She booked us into a grand hotel in the colonial hill station of Dalhousie. We each had a palatial four-poster bed with a dressing room, large bathroom and veranda leading onto the gardens and magnificent views of misty hills and valleys below us. We went horse riding and globe rolling, which is like being a guinea pig in a perspex ball.

One night, the hotel lit a large fire and turned on a ghetto blaster. Irene dragged me up to dance as sparks flew up into the black sky. We spun to the words of Barbie Girl – "I'm a Barbie girl in a Barbie world." It was simple fun, which was what Irene wanted and needed. I did, too, but I wasn't very good at it. My limbs flapped, awkward and clunky. Above us, stars twinkled their blessings.

When we met the revered head of this lineage, I prostrated respectfully. Irene strode forward and, to his astonishment, extended her hand. Her handshake was strong. From my prone position on the floor, I saw him wince.

Afterwards, in the taxi, she said, 'He's a human being, like me. Nice to meet him, but he didn't even offer tea.' I liked her style.

Irene was training me stealthily, tactfully and tenderly. One birthday she took me for lunch at a swanky restaurant with a wonderful view. Another time she booked me a pamper session and massage. She hauled me around on a shopping trip to Manchester, and to my shame, I judged her silently for spending £300 on face cream. Looking back, I realise she knew she had a year or less to live. She was trying to be loving to herself. I hadn't known how imminent her final exit was.

For Christmas, she gave me stained glass ornaments she'd made, one of them a model of my black cat. When she saw my large white granny pants, she was exasperated. When she heard they were my mother-in-law's (three brand new at the back of her cupboard when she died – what was a girl to do?) she was shocked. She organised the yoga class to club together to give me a voucher for fancy underwear for Christmas. One day after yoga she had a steely look in her eye and told me to follow her car to a retail centre. She refused to listen to my protests. I came out with the fluffiest towel for swimming and a thousand percentile cotton sheets for my bed. Each time I use that towel (I swim three times a week), and each time I slip into my cosy bed with its soft caressing sheets, my understanding of what it means to be truly kind and caring to oneself increases.

Early that spring, I walked into the yoga class and looked around.

'Where is Irene?' I asked.

No one knew. She was never late for yoga. I rang her when I got home.

'I fell yesterday, down the stairs. Don't worry, I've just bruised myself. My ribs won't stop hurting.'

I was worried.

'Go to your doctor today. Now. Ask them to check you. Please.'

At the doctors' they scanned her. The cancer was back. It had spread to her rib cage, spine and some internal organs. The best they could do to delay the horrible outcome was to give her chemotherapy. Even then I knew I was buffering. I had to buffer. I couldn't let myself hear her clearly. I feared it would cause enormous cracks that would radiate out and break me.

My valiant friend kept attending yoga. In a downward dog, her chemo wig fell off and she threw it towards me. I had to try it on. It was much better than my own hair. Irene took either to wearing a scarf or simply being bald. She lost her eyebrows and said every hair on her body had gone, so at least she didn't have to shave her legs any more. I was allowed to admit my envy.

A few more months flew by. Then she stopped turning up to yoga, so I would drop by her home after the class. We sat on her enormous sofa, one at each end, our legs stretched out towards each other, tangled up, toes tickling, a blanket over our feet. That sofa became like a boat in the stormy sea that was both our lives. I was at the beginning of a massive breakdown – or breakthrough – and working with Joe, my psychologist. Irene always wanted to know how the session had gone that week. We hugged our mugs of tea and shared our most difficult secrets and shames. When, haltingly, I told her my worst shame of all, she somehow managed to have me laughing about it by my second cup of tea.

She didn't come to my fiftieth birthday party. She sent a message saying she was tired. I was upset. In my complicated, wounded way of relating to people, it suggested I didn't matter. Without realising it, I backed off a little that autumn, even though I still visited her and we sailed the seas in our boat, even past the fading of the light, when Irene reluctantly got up and put on a lamp, so the magic of our secret floating world continued into the evening.

My soul still felt heavy at my petulant moods. I never voiced those moods but I'm sure she felt them, sensing that I was like the meerkat on the edge of the pack, ostracised when the pack closed ranks and carried on with their lives regardless of me.

My childhood was like that. Like a crazy moth battering at a flame, I kept trying to make myself matter to my parents. As a result, small things that might indicate I don't matter to someone still wound me deeply, as though my wings and body were burning in the candle flame. "Don't take it so seriously," people tell me.

In July, Irene was a little tired. During the autumn, she asked people not to drop by. We chatted on Facebook instead. At the yoga class, I admitted I didn't know how she was; her husband had given me no news, and I didn't like to intrude. My students urged me to visit the house immediately after the class. Thank goodness they did. Her husband opened the door, distraught.

'They've taken her into hospital. She was vomiting all night and in tremendous pain. She's very ill.'

'Which hospital, Steve? Tell me where she is!'

I tried not to drive too fast. When I walked into the ward, she was propped up in bed: no hair, swollen belly, pale, bloated blotchy face.

'Oh, Sarah, thank God. Thank God you're here.'

I wanted to wrap her in a blanket of love and tenderness. I wanted to rock her with soothing words and gentle caresses. I wanted to pick her up and run out of there with her. Run to safety. Her body seemed almost luminescent. Her eyes were wide, and her hands clutched the bed sheet. She asked me about death and dying.

'I don't know. I truly don't know. I guess it could be like before we were born?'

We reminisced about the good times.

'You two must be sisters,' said a nurse passing by. She'd seen us laughing until we cried. Irene looked at me.

'No,' she said. 'She is NOT my sister.' Pause. I deflated. 'No,' she went on, 'she's more than a sister to me.'

Rather tentatively, she asked me if I would help her with the bedpan. She was finding it hard to pee, yet she needed to try.

Rather shakily, she said, 'Remember when Linda and I had the shits on the train back to Delhi, and we joked that those harem pants with elastic at the ankles were the only thing that stopped it hitting the floor?'

She laughed with childlike glee. It was hard not to join in. Yes, I remembered.

'Well, what's a bedpan between soul sisters?' she grinned.

I helped her on and cleaned her up, and when her tears fell with pain and exhaustion, I kissed each one, kissing them away. Salty sweet.

When her family turned up, Steve whispered, 'Can we have some time, just us? Can you come back tomorrow?'

I gave her a kiss and a hug and reluctantly walked out to the nurses' station. I asked if they were planning to move her to a hospice as it was distressing to see her in a busy general ward when she needed quiet and peace. They said they were going to move her in the morning. I looked back at her bed. She appeared exposed and cross, but mostly deadly weary. At 10 am the following day, my phone rang.

Steve said, 'I'm sorry, but she died at 5:30 this morning.'

The shock made my knees melt. My mouth emitted strange howls. My body slipped to the floor, one hand scrabbling to grip the hallway wall. My fingers looked like they were trying to tap out some message, but all they wanted to do was stop the world from tilting.

'No! No, she can't be, she can't. No!'

Maybe you know that moment. A physical punch to the gut, a dagger in the heart, the strings of the body cut as we fall like a collapsed puppet. But she'd "slipped away". That's what they say, as though it's something gentle. She'd been unmoored, sailed down the slipway and gone to sail other oceans. She had escaped this boiling sea of pain and indignity, diarrhoea and vomiting, wasting away – the brutal agony of the final few months.

Steve invited me to be the celebrant for her funeral. I remember walking down the aisle with her body in the coffin behind me. I didn't think I'd make it to the front.

A few weeks later, he asked me to sort out her clothes and possessions. He told me to take anything of hers I could use or wear. So I ended up with those expensive face creams, her best coat, a few of her books, two exquisite bras; but no granny pants.

Steve also insisted on paying me for being the celebrant though I retorted that it was the least I could do for my Irene. Nevertheless, a cheque arrived in the post for just under £200. I used it to buy the boots.

Back in Choir, my feet were creating larger wet pools on the wooden floor. It was nearly time for the choir tea break and I'd have to brazen it out. 'Regroup at 9:10,' instructed our conductor. I moved fast to get near the front of the tea queue and someone tapped my shoulder.

'You're leaving wet footprints.'

I looked. There was a clear line, almost a slug trail, across the floor behind me. Smiling, I replied, 'It's my superpower.' I wanted a hot drink mostly for its soothing qualities but I knew it would increase the dripping. Snippets of conversation swarmed around me. I was too hot. I was thirsty. I was upset about my boots. I'd only wanted warm feet. Clutching my cup and bourbon biscuit I headed for a quiet spot.

'Sarah! How's it going?'

'Oh, fine.'

'You look flustered.' My choir buddy Jackie had been standing next to me all rehearsal and had seen the tugging and followed my paw prints. 'I've been watching you put on your cardigan and take it off and put it on again for some months now. Have you ever, by any chance, considered you may be going through menopause? Because I was just like that when it was happening to me.'

Menopause? I was too young. Hell and botheration, I was only fifty. Well, fifty and a half. It couldn't be happening to me. Rhona came over and noticed my face.

'Oh, Sarah! Hey, don't cry! Come on, come and sit out in the foyer with me. Come on, bring your tea.'

At least it was cool out there. I settled down on one of the comfy chairs.

'Spill it out. Go on. I'm a good listener.'

Maybe it would help.

'You know Irene, my friend who died in November last year, 2011? You know how she was my dearest loveliest friend? She was the kindest, most perceptive, most tender, generous and wise person I've ever had as a close friend.'

'Well, that's a strange way to make a friend like me feel special.'

I laughed ruefully. I felt her hand on my shoulder.

'It's so hard to lose someone.'

'It is! It was only last Easter that I dared admit to Irene that I actually felt love for her. She was my much loved, cherished and trusted friend. You know, when I told her, she laughed, hugged me and said, "Of course. I love you too". Loving her felt so easy. She was safe, she was kind, and she was so able to just be herself.'

I was crying again and trying to manage by wiping my face on my sleeve because my tears were plopping onto my shirt.

'You can go home if you want,' said Rhona.

'But I left my boots in choir – the boots that I bought because Irene had encouraged me, no, told me to take care, kind care of myself, and also to make sure my feet don't get so bloody cold.'

Rhona looked at me. Her eyes moistened and she took my hand.

'Go home. I'll get your boots and your bag. I'll say you have a headache.'

Of course, it was raining as I drove home. I'd been getting migraines during the previous four or five years, some of them off the scale in pain. I was experiencing tremendous mood swings, deep despairs and a feeling of bleakness and worthlessness, which made life seem pointless. My brain was fogging up and I was finding it hard to sleep because I got so hot at night and was fatigued. Joe the psychologist said it was all trauma symptoms.

I visualised Irene in my passenger seat.

Me: "Irene, neither of us spotted it. I was perimenopausal. All those symptoms, none of them seemed anything but me going into a terrible breakdown. I felt too young to even begin to think of menopause. It never entered my head."

Irene: "Sweetie, Don't beat yourself up. Go and see your GP. Get a referral to a menopause clinic ASAP... And get some HRT."

All of which I did. The symptoms subsided dramatically. My boots became cosy rather than swelteringly hot. They became my trademark footwear from October to April. The prickle of guilt and shame for not being there enough for Irene during her last awful few months began to lessen as I realised, with more self-compassion, that I'd been more than overwhelmed during that time, drowning but not understanding how out of my depth I was. I'd kept hiding it behind a false smile, pushing myself even when I had nothing left. I'd known she was on chemo; but chemo works, right?

Cabins Apart
by Delia Louise Seville

'Fasten your seat belt, please Madam,' said the attractive air hostess, as she did her final checks.

I was nervous about the flight and her confident manner comforted me.

'Oh yes, sorry,' I replied.

I fumbled for the straps, trying hard not to invade the gentleman's space on my left. A strong aroma of hot chilli spices and garlic wafted across my face. One good thing about an aisle seat was that I could get up during the long flight without disturbing anyone.

The Boeing 787 taxied down the runway. Reality dawned on me. Oh my God, what am I doing? There is no turning back now. An adventure mixed with excitement and fear.

Less than an hour ago, only thirty-five minutes before take-off, I was at the China Airways customer services desk, happily assuming, secretly hoping, there'd be no seats left. There was one – a return ticket at the cost of a whopping nine hundred pounds – and it was mine. With Russell towering over me and smiling, I felt trapped.

'Hurry,' said the assistant, 'the gate closes for boarding in five minutes – you will have to run.'

En route, I phoned my son.

Thankfully he answered, with his usual cheerful, 'Hello Mum?'

'Hi, Tom,' I drew a deep breath.

'Oh, hi. Is everything okay? We're looking forward to seeing you on Christmas Day.'

With no time to feel guilty, it spilt out unrehearsed.

'That's why I'm calling. I'm really sorry Tom but I won't be coming. Change of plan. I've been invited on a cruise and I'm at Heathrow now, literally about to board a plane to Singapore to pick up the ship.'

'A cruise? Singapore? What? Did I hear you right?' He chuckled.

'Yes,' I replied, clearing my throat as perspiration ran down my brow. 'A cruise.'

'Really? That's crazy. Well, have a great time and take care. We'll miss you. Oh, and who are you going with?'

Panting, I managed to reply.

'Roz, you know, my friend from work. She was let down at the last minute. Spare ticket. Let's catch up when I get back in seven days. Love you. Bye.'

I knew Tom would have been horrified if he'd known the truth. Besides, I didn't want to hear him tell me what I would have said to my mother. Especially if she appeared to be having a late midlife crisis. I felt ashamed telling him a white lie.

We stepped onto the plane to be greeted by a sea of faces, staring. Were they annoyed that we were the cause of the delayed departure?

Smooth take-off. I opened my eyes. London was fading fast beneath me. I was seated far apart from Russell – grateful to have that space. My sleeping neighbour had a rhythmic snore and looked content, oblivious of his surroundings. I looked past him out of the tiny window; the sky resembled swirling cloud-like smoke being exhaled out of a monster's nostril. Trying to relax, too alert to sleep, I took out my jotter and pen from my shoulder bag. I needed to write to keep track of my senses and at least try to justify my impulsive adolescent-like behaviour; my mind raced but my pen froze.

Forty-eight hours ago, I had been dreading the thought of Christmas and celebrations. The returning home to silent walls and emptiness, and the loneliness that creeps into the anti-climax. Feelings of redundancy as a mother and wife – the children now parents themselves – and the cheating ex-husband on his third wife… I sighed.

Glancing around the plane, I saw people chatting and smiling, imagining them returning home to loved ones, with their stories to tell. The elegant air hostess came by with little tongs bearing warm, soft, damp wipes – a sweet-smelling relief. I liked her reassuring smile.

I grinned to myself thinking back to when my friend Josephine had egged me on to sign up for online dating. She was a man-magnet with her high cheekbones, long, dark, silky hair and Barbie-doll figure. We had become a little tipsy that evening as we lamented the idea of ending up as "old maids" in our later years.

'It's the only way forward, you know… look at me,' she slurred, as she took another gulp of wine and flopped her head onto her folded arms on the tabletop.

'Never in a million years,' I murmured. 'Not my thing.'

At two o'clock in the morning, alone at home. What the heck, I thought, as I signed up for a free month's trial on Encounters, the dating site she had recommended. What's there to lose?

I made a rule to never include a photo of myself on my profile, but to always require a photo from any potential suitor. I knew that photos could be out-of-date and misleading, but I thought I could at least get the gist of the person.

I can't recall who initiated contact first, whether it was me or Russell, but it all began with an online wink. From there, the typical process involves a series of phone conversations over the course of several days or even weeks, which might eventually lead to a proper face-to-face date.

On our initial telephone chat, Russell told me he was going away the next day, the day before Christmas Eve. It had become his norm as he had no family or friends to spend the festive season with. The chat went well so we agreed to meet for an unusually fast-tracked first date that evening at Brown's in Windsor, a trendy, upmarket riverside restaurant.

Russell was already seated at a candlelit table for two in the middle of the hot, crowded room. He was easy to spot from his photo and was the only lone diner. It was a romantic setting, with a spectacularly decorated tree, twinkling lights all around, and *"Have yourself a merry little Christmas"* playing through the loudspeakers. I was glad for the dim lights and hoped no one was there who might recognise me because this arrangement felt so unnatural to me.

My first impression of the real article was this six-foot-two Chris Tarrant look-a-like with a full head of creamy-white hair, pale eyelashes, and vivid blue eyes. Well educated and fit from playing squash at his club (three times a week, he told me). His after-shave smelt expensive and his red cashmere jumper seemed to reflect a rosy glow on his cheeks.

Our casual banter flowed as we finished the starters and went onto the mains. He told me he had a lucrative job in IT and was divorced with no children. Both his parents had died quite a while ago and he had no siblings. He said he didn't wish to impose himself on any of his few married friends, so he planned his yearly getaway in the sun, always on the twenty-third of December.

It was easy for me to empathise with his situation at Christmas time. I told him a little about myself, carefully holding back as much as I could. By dessert, we were freely exchanging like-minded views on adventure and spontaneity, when suddenly, after he'd ordered another glass of red wine, the question came up.

'I've got a brilliant idea, why don't you come on the cruise with me? I can check if there are any cabins left first thing in the morning. My treat. You just pay for your flight.' He looked down into his trifle.

Surely it must be the wine talking?

'Um,' I gulped down more of my mineral water, 'but we've only just met…'

'I'm not asking you to share a cabin. It would just be nice to have company at the dinner table, a change from eating alone, and we seem to get on well.'

I was tempted. My sense of adventure and charitable heartstrings were being pulled and I understood his feelings about the festive season. Besides, I had never been on a cruise and it seemed almost mean to refuse his kind offer and let him go alone.

'I guess there's no harm in seeing if it's possible, as long as it's understood we are two lonely souls embarking on a strictly companionship week away.'

'Of course,' he said, turning his head and waving across to the waiter to order coffee.

There was definitely no chemistry there for me, but it felt like a reasonable idea at the time.

Dinner was over, and Russell would not allow me to share the bill. We politely said our goodnights at the door, agreeing that in the morning he would ask the cruise company to call me with any availability and I would try to book myself on the same flight as him if that was possible…

The telephone woke me early from a turbulent night's sleep.

'Hello, Mrs Seville? It's Costa Cruises here. I'm Michelle. How are you today? Mr Russell Clarke has booked you an inside cabin on the Costa Fortuna for seven nights, from Singapore to Malaysia and Thailand.'

'Oh, good morning. Um, I'm not really sure how I am actually. Will he be able to get a refund if I can't get a flight? It's such short notice and with Christmas Eve being tomorrow, it seems very unlikely.'

'Yes, that won't be a problem; I've put it on hold until confirmed. It's a cabin on the same deck as him, will that be okay for you?'

I gasped as a sense of panic went through my body.

'Hello? Are you still there?' Michelle enquired, jogging me back to my senses.

'NO, no, not okay, that's not a good plan at all, but thank you,' I said to her.

My spontaneous, rude-sounding "no" led me to be honest and open with Michelle. I told her about the first date yesterday evening and the proposed arrangement. She seemed both amused and in awe of my courage, eagerly aiding and abetting my request for a cabin as far away from Russell as possible. I also paid a hundred pounds extra for an outside cabin, next to a lift, four decks above his. She wished me luck and giggled goodbye.

A text came through from Russell.

'Will park at yours. Ordered a taxi for 4 pm to take us to Heathrow. Hope you got the flight booked by now, I haven't heard from you?'

It seemed surreal and exciting but also ridiculous to be going on a cruise with a stranger.

I texted back. 'No. Still trying. Will keep you in the loop.'

Josephine had called and instead of encouraging me out of this scenario, she'd egged me on even more.

'Oh, how lucky are you? Why doesn't that happen to me? I'm so envious, you would be stupid not to go, I will be with you in spirit all the way.'

My head was telling me that this shouldn't be happening, but my weak-willed self was still going through the motions of calling cheap flight agencies. They were unhelpful and time-consuming, and I took it as a sign that it wasn't meant to be. With a sigh of relief, I thought to myself, 'It's not happening,' and my stomach stopped aching.

The loud tooting horn outside told me it must be four o'clock. I looked out the window. Russell was waving, standing by a taxi. He shouted out to me,

'Come on, the flight won't wait.'

He'd already transferred his Samsonite Neopulse Spinner luggage out of his red Porsche and into the boot of the taxi. Panic-stricken, I shouted back.

'Oh, is that the time? Sorry to let you down Russell, but I've had no luck with getting a flight, so you will have to go without me. But you can still leave your car there.'

'Quick, just pack any bag. You can get tickets directly at the airport. If not, you can come back in a taxi. You've nothing to lose. Remember your passport, come on we're running late.'

'Oh, er… OK. Give me five minutes.' I shut the window feeling guilty and annoyed that I had not called him back and that he had assumed I had booked a flight.

Grabbing the only receptacle I could find, a holdall I used mainly for the gym, I rushed to my wardrobe to seek out any remotely summery clothes. Hardly anything. Same with the cash in my purse. I rummaged through my drawer and found my passport. My head was in a spin and my adrenaline was running high. I checked around – windows shut, and electrics off. Grabbing my daily jotter – my security blanket – I slid it into my shoulder bag and cast a final glance behind me before leaving the house.

As I sat in the taxi beside this man, I was still counting on the likelihood that I wouldn't get a ticket, considering it was only a couple of hours until take-off and many families would be flying home for the Christmas holidays.

Russell looked different from last night. His pale complexion was more dimpled, with a fresh shaving rash and a small, round, waterproof plaster insecurely attached to his chin. His bright-yellow windproof bomber jacket, orange check tee-shirt, tight white jeans, and dazzling new white trainers were not appealing to me at all. Nor was the constant clearing of his throat and picking his nose with his thumb and forefinger.

Still, it's just companionship, I kept telling myself…

We landed. I put away my jotter and pen and got ready to disembark. My neighbour woke up, nodded and smiled revealing three lone nicotine-stained teeth in his mouth.

Singapore was the cleanest city I had ever seen. The cruise ship, a giant floating hotel that looked almost too big for its berth, was waiting at the International Cruise Terminal next to the Marina South Pier under the clear blue sky and sunshine. The warm air on my face made me forget about the gloomy grey skies and cold that we had left behind.

We had been transported to a beautiful world of lush, green palm trees, pristine pavements, and sun-tanned men dressed in crisp white outfits trimmed with gold braid. These men, wearing smart white caps greeted us with flashing bright smiles and gleaming white teeth as we began to board the ship.

Russell appeared more than a little dismayed that our cabins were far apart and seemed envious that I had acquired an outside one. Giving him my cabin number was never going to be an option, even though he asked many times when he could come and see it. I also politely declined his frequent offers to visit his cabin.

I discovered that in my great rush to pack a bag, I'd not even thought to include any toiletries. That was daft but understandable under the circumstances. I made do with the complementary ones in my cabin until our first shore stop, up the coast, at a small, basic, Malaysian shopping mall.

'Russell, I really need to do some girlie shopping. How about I meet you for a coffee over at that bar in say, thirty minutes, my treat before we go back to the ship?'

'I'll come with you,' he insisted.

'No, I'm fine thanks, I'd rather go by myself,'

'But I'd like to come,' he began to walk towards me.

'No really – no need. Besides, you'll be bored.'

'Give me a kiss before you go,' he demanded, his face heading down towards my lips.I turned my head sharply to offer my cheek, surprised at his sudden forwardness.

'Is that all I get?' he said with a scowl. I sped off through the mall, not looking back.

What part of "companionship" did Russell not understand? I didn't wish for any awkwardness between us. I took a slow sip of my espresso to give me time to concoct a convincing reason for rejecting his advances.

'I've realised, Russell, that I'm just not ready for a new romantic relationship, even if George Clooney were to come knocking at my door.' (I didn't want to hurt his feelings, but felt it best said there and then, in case I had accidentally given him any false hopes.)

Russell looked into space. His one word reply, "Interesting" gave me goosebumps. I hoped he'd really heard me this time and not taken it personally.

Back on board, we parted, agreeing to meet at our dinner table at eight pm.

Russell sat there avoiding eye contact, instead mostly looking past me through the massive window at the ocean rolling by.

'I can see why people get hooked on cruising,' I tried to open up the conversation.

'Interesting,' he said, again. This was turning into his stock one-word response to anything I said. It felt odd and annoying.

There were no after-dinner drinks, 'I've got a headache,' he proclaimed.

'See you for Christmas morning breakfast then?' I almost whispered, as we headed out of the dining room. He did not reply. We went our separate ways.

Six days later, the return journey.

The friendly young man at the airline check-in offered me a choice of available cabin seats on the plane. Luckily, there was one at the farthest end of the plane from Russell's pre-booked seat. The long flight gave me a chance to reflect on and write up the past few days in my jotter... I began where I left off.

Christmas Eve. I found it hard to sleep. 2 am: went up to the top-deck shop and decided to buy Russell a Christmas present as everybody deserves to wake up on Christmas morning with at least one gift. Made wrapping out of ships' serviettes for the just affordable, pure silk tie. Used a blue hair ribbon. to tie around it. Hope he likes it. Eventually, I fell asleep.

Christmas Day. Went to breakfast with slight anticipation and excitement with the delicately wrapped present. Sat there alone for an hour, feeling embarrassed, and foolish. I hoped no one else noticed.

Sent a text, 'Happy Christmas Russell, must have missed you at breakfast?'

Wandered around decks, English Christmas songs were blaring out of the speakers. People were jumping in and out of the pools, splashing and having fun. Lump in my throat. Held back the tears. Hard to connect to the feel of a Christmas day. A sudden sadness came over me.

12.30 – Buffet lunch. No Russell. No text. Sat and watched the calm ocean roll by, my mind drifting to Christmases past when I was once part of a happy family scene. My cheeks felt wet, not just from the ocean spray.

2 pm – Went to the lounge, sat watching loving families and couples laughing. Tried to stop my mind drifting back to home; the family, roasting turkey, carols, and crackers, even Josephine. It's too painful to phone Tom yet.

4 pm – Worried. Perhaps Russell is lying dead in his cabin? He looked pale yesterday. Asked the service desk to call his room.

'No reply, Madame. Sorry, I will try again later. Sure, all is fine'.

Why should I care?

It's hard not to. Wouldn't any compassionate human being?

5 pm – Circled the ship. No Russell. Sat and people-watched. Feeling lonely.

6 pm – Informed that Russell was alive as he had now answered reception on his cabin phone. Returned to my cabin with the present and got changed for dinner.

7.30 pm – Sat outside lift by the dining room. Trying to smile and look happy to the passers-by.

8.30 pm – Lift doors open. Only Russell walks out. Pale face now as sore-red as an English pillar box! No words were exchanged on the way to the dining room… Pushed the pressie across the table and enquired where he'd been all day.

'I have been sunbathing on the exercise deck, where it is the highest and the least crowded,' he said matter-of-factly.

I was angry with myself for the waste of a day worrying about him and angrier with him that he had not had the good grace to tell me whatever his reason for playing Mr Invisible had been. It was mean and rude. Very little conversation ensued. Interesting! After dinner, we went our separate ways with no thanks at all for the tie, maybe not his colour.

Boxing Day. On-shore trip to Bangkok. No Russell. Thank goodness for a kind, pleasant, German lady, Greta and her two teenagers Heinz and Dagmar. Invited to join them to share a taxi and sight-see. We had all missed out on tickets for the ship's organised coach party. Took exhilarating water taxi along the over-crowded, swirling muddy river to the enormous mountainside Golden Buddha. Couldn't make the one hundred steep steps; took photos of Dagmar and Heinz. Bought souvenirs in the market. Ate Thai for the first time, liked it. Back to ship and drank cocktails, danced in the evening. Talked with Greta about adventures past and our lives now. Told her about Russell. She thinks I have made him up, a fictitious story. As if …

December 27. On-shore trip with Greta, Heinz and Dagmar to Koh Samui. Taxi was like an old, battered baked bean can with rickety wheels. Roads chaotic, noisy with horns blowing from every direction. Bought a blue and white sarong for the palm-fringed sandy beach. The calming waves lapped onto the shore. Peddlers heavily laden, adorned in trinkets and fake jewels passed by.

Last two days at sea. Sunbathed on deck with family. Russell unexpectedly appeared wearing tight orange Speedos, with a bright yellow Ralph Lauren beach towel slung over his beetroot-red torso. After a throwaway "hello" he sped past without waiting for a reply. For a moment we all stared in amazement.

'You see there really is a Russell; how could I have made it up?' I said.

They burst out laughing, 'Oh Mein Gott! Is he for real?'

Glad Christmas is over. Called Tom before docking.

'Hi Tom. How are you all? Sorry I couldn't call you before, no signal.'

'That's okay Mum, nice to hear you. We missed you. Kids loved their presents. Raining here. Have you been having a great time?' – The signal was bad and the call cut out…

Smooth landing. Back to grey skies, and rain. I waited while Russell collected his luggage.

There was a cold, uncomfortable atmosphere in the taxi. Only the driver offered any conversation.

The taxi dropped us off and left us standing there. Russell loaded his cases into the car in silence. I stretched out my arm to shake his hand. He stood staring at me with his hands on his hips, not responding to my gesture and giving me an arrogant look.

'You actually owe me five hundred pounds for the cabin, you know. I will email my bank details to you tomorrow and expect it to be in my account by night.'

Taken aback, I asked respectfully, 'What do you mean?' I felt those goose pimples again.

'Well, for starters, I expected far more than just a kiss on the cheek…' he said in an indignant little-boy tone.

He opened the door of the Porsche and sat in the driver's seat staring straight ahead. After a few revs of the engine he sped away down the drive.

I wasn't sure how I felt about our parting. It really had been an adventure and one that I would never forget. My German family and I promised to keep in touch – without them the week would have been a sad disaster. As for Encounters, Russell was my one and only date and I did not hear from him again. Josephine, on the other hand, is still on the dating site in hopes of a Christmas (or any) cruise! She knows that I'm back in "never-in-a-million-years" land.

Bottled Up Emotions
by Chassie Stone

Capricorns: the ultimate worker bees. They're ambitious, organised, practical, goal-oriented, and they don't mind the hustle. They're ready to give up a lot in order to achieve their goals. They also love living by their own rules which means they strive to reach high career positions. Her star sign.

The letter was cruel, cutting, and uncompromising. Handwritten in her tiny, crab-like scrawl she laid out the cold facts – she was never loved and her feelings were never taken into account.

Stabbed through my heart and that was just the opening lines. Could I bear to continue reading? Heart pounding now, mouth dry, I squinted at the writing trying to decipher the words and meaning. It continued relentlessly, that basically, I was nonexistent to her during her childhood and indifferent to her needs. Wow, the easy way out is to write a vile letter and never see the person face to face.

Actually, that is harsh, it is difficult to write a vile letter and sometimes it is the only way of expressing pent-up emotions. Maybe wiser to follow up with a face-to-face meeting? Perhaps the facts had turned into hatred over the years and now, safely married and in her early thirties she could finally put down in words what she had longed to say all of her life.

I had to stop reading. I pictured her, at her desk, sun streaming in, illuminating her hair with a golden streak. Writing this letter, expression neutral, using her pen as a finely sharpened scalpel, to skilfully insert and lift off layers of repressed emotions. All laid bare, unforgiving.

Guilt and shame washed over me. Tears, sobbing, lots of. Is that really what my only daughter thought of me, a totally uncaring, unloving mother? She even had a dig at the difference in spirituality. She is a fervent born-again Christian and I'm an Interfaith and Spiritualist sort of person. At least I am a believer – doesn't that count in her book? Apparently not.

Every aspect of her youth was dissected in a precise summing up of her "horrible childhood" including holidays which she hated and claimed she was never consulted about. Especially camping, as she called it, in our motor caravan. She admitted that I cared for her financially, and she was able to join in with all of the school overseas trips including Russia and to the USA. Even my friends were included in her cutting analysis, especially the male ones including my partner. Nothing was spared. After she had stripped me bare and lashed me to bits with her pen, she went on to slay my mother.

In my defence, I had been single, living with my mother. I had to work to support all of us. Mother adored the baby and was there for her. An overprotective guardian angel, but there for her. My mother could be difficult and had stubborn ways of control, never compromising an inch.

The difficulty increased as my daughter started school, and wanted to learn to swim – pools were filthy and not allowed. I had to step in, insisted I'd find a cleaner swimming centre where my daughter could learn. Children have friends and like to visit each other's homes and stay over. That was not allowed. There was always tension and arguments, me trying to loosen the iron control my mother exerted. Then, when my daughter was nine years old, mother died. She viciously pointed the sword at my mother's memory – she had no kind feelings whatsoever for her.

My guts felt torn as if I were giving birth again only it was my soul being ripped out. Disorientated, I told myself I would wake up and find it was a joke or a nightmare. But it wasn't. There it was, in black and white, just there, where I had left it.

Who was this person accusing me? Just six months before I had given her away at her wedding to a man I hardly knew, but who seemed to love her as she did him. Why the intense animosity? What provoked this outburst? My head was pounding now, I couldn't think, so tired but I knew I wouldn't be able to sleep. Far too ashamed to discuss the contents with anyone, I hid the letter. Feeling used and bruised I had to leave the house for a long walk. Breathe deep, keep breathing – my meditation to keep me going. I forget to breathe when stressed. I told my husband on my return. 'Serves you right, you can be an old cow bag sometimes.' Flippant as usual. Then he looked at me properly and realised that this was huge.

'I'm sure she doesn't mean it.'

'Of course she bloody means it otherwise she wouldn't have written it,' I yelled at him and stalked off, shaking again. The waves of humiliation, anger, hurt, love and hate were just too much. A bottle of wine, or two, or three or… could wash away some of the pain.

I couldn't read any more. The words became meaningless and my mangled brain couldn't take it. Put the letter away, forget about it, she'll ring you.

After two weeks, no phone call. Still feeling wretched, confiding in my friend, showing her the letter.

I hate confrontation. I will have to write back begging forgiveness. She put on her glasses and began to read. Ten long minutes, as she kept re-reading, saying that the small writing was difficult to see.

'My goodness, this is savage. What on earth has brought this on? Have you two had an argument?'

I shook my head, 'We've not spoken since the wedding. They went on honeymoon and returned to work. She sent me a birthday card in September saying we'd have to arrange something for Christmas. Now, this.'

She read it again. 'I think she is jealous.' She read out a sentence that could mean something else.

'I don't think so, from the tone of the letter she despises me. I will have to answer this, apologise, grovel, try to explain and answer her accusations. I just can't ignore it. She never does anything on the spur of the moment. This has been bubbling for a long time.'

She came over and hugged me. 'I am so sorry, I really don't know what to say.'

The father she never knew. Maybe that was the problem. The missing link in her life. I never married him. Various reasons but I craved freedom. Her being wasn't a result of teenage fumbles. A love child from a failed relationship. When he heard I was pregnant he did give me a choice. Marry or get rid of it. That wasn't a romantic proposal. My mother disliked him. He said I was tied to her apron strings. Trouble was, she was tied to me. She could never be abandoned, she would sink like a stricken ship unable to steer all alone. He expected her to buy us our home, to set us up and disappear. That wasn't going to happen. I would have the baby and put it up for adoption. Nobody would know, no one knew I was pregnant.

Mother and I lived in Madrid. Our house, our home was there. I worked for a British airline as an accountant. I met him at a work party at Heathrow. Love beckoned and I put in for a transfer to work in the UK. Initially, I stayed with workmates then my mother came and we rented a flat in Ealing. Life and love blossomed until the fateful pregnancy test. The plan was to have the baby, arrange for the adoption agency to take it, and we would return home. But plans can go wrong. Mother and I fell in love with the baby and that was that, she was ours.

If he had contacted me, I would have compromised, done as much as I could to create a family nest. Even when I took him to court for maintenance, I waited for a sign, to profess his undying love. Although he knew he had a baby daughter he denied it was his. There was no going back, only forward. When she was about fifteen years old she wanted to contact him. I got an address for him and she wrote him a letter. He replied, enclosing a photo and a brief summary of his life. In addition, he just had to mention he didn't think he was her father. He was married but didn't have any children.

She took it well, seemed happy she'd made a connection and left it at that.

My daughter always saw life happening in black and white. There were no grey areas. Once she had made up her mind that she didn't want a friendship or anyone in her life that wasn't like her, she would break the link. So much like my mother, they never went back on their decisions.

I wrote back, apologising, expressing hurt that she couldn't have been more open with me. I thought we had been honest with each other. Begged her to meet me, somewhere neutral, to really talk, shout, and scream if necessary. Her answer was another short, cold, concise, hateful letter.

Twenty years have passed, and I am totally cancelled out of her life. I am reconciled to that. Our children are gifts to us, to protect and nurture but they don't belong to us. No one belongs to anyone. When ties are cut, that's that. I appreciate that I gave birth to a beautiful girl and did the very best I could for her. I am not perfect - I made mistakes, but she was the centre of my life and my reason for living. It wasn't enough, it wasn't meant to last. My purgatory, her freedom. She is a true Capricorn.

Opening the Door
by Micki Findlay

No one warned me how lonely marriage can be.

How did I get here? Pregnant at seventeen. Trapped in a remote town with a man I don't love. Desperately missing the island where I lived nearly all my life. The winters here are relentless and the isolation unbearable. Some days I find it hard to breathe. Other days, I'm not sure I want to.

This is not what I'd planned for my life.

Stumbling blindly in a maze of emotional adolescence, he and I are lost in a world neither of us chose to be in. I can just imagine his iron-fisted father berating him…

"Son, this is *your* mess, not mine. *You* knocked her up. *Deal with it!*"

The proposal, if you can call it that, happened at a New Year's Eve party in his sister's basement. I can't recall the words – only his coal-black beard glistening with driblets of rye whiskey – his breath reeking of cigarettes. I heard myself agreeing in trance-like detachment, as if in a nightmare – one in which you wake up feeling ill but aren't quite sure why. The song, *Lyin' Eyes*, by the Eagles, echoed in the walls as if mocking us. Or was it a warning? Either way, it would prove to be chillingly prophetic.

The next morning I woke up alone, anxious, my swollen belly churning with morning sickness. Something inside me cried out, *Don't do this! It's a mistake!* But I wasn't accustomed to listening to my own voice, let alone trusting it. Besides, what choice did I have – a minimum-wage waitress with no post-secondary education? At sixteen, I'd run away from home and had no intention of crawling back. *Anything* but that.

Maybe I could learn to love this man. After all, he was committed to me and our unborn child, even if he seemed emotionally detached. But it was on our wedding night, in a smoke-stained hotel, when the full weight of reality ripped open the veil of optimism. The stranger who lay beside me was miles away. Feeling utterly alone, I stared up at the amber-crusted ceiling; my head throbbing, my mind racing. *What had I done?*

The radiant bride, just hours earlier, was now crying herself to sleep.

So, here we are, nearly two years later. Little has changed, except that we have a house and a beautiful, one-year-old son. And, God help me, another baby on the way. I have no idea how to be a mother. Nurturing does not come naturally to me, and I'm certain I'm failing miserably. Not knowing where to turn, I express my fears to my husband. He tells me to stop being ridiculous. I never mention it again.

Even now, we rarely talk, unless he's angry. I'm a non-entity; a bug to be swatted when it flies too close. Until nighttime when, suddenly, my presence is welcome – the only time he lets me in. I feel used but it's all I have, so I don't let on. When he's done, I cry into my pillow, hoping he won't notice the bed shaking.

When did I become this small, sad version of myself?

I'm reminded of the song playing in his sister's basement…

Late at night a big old house gets lonely, I guess every form of refuge has its price.
And it breaks her heart to think her love is only, given to a man with hands as cold as ice.
You can't hide those lyin' eyes…

Except… I can.

Desperately yearning to be seen, appreciated – loved, I find myself attracted to other men. Men who listen to me. Men who talk to me. Men who don't see me as the vexing doormat one is forever tripping on. One man in particular. A man who offers warmth in this frozen purgatory.

A man I've given my body to… twice.

For a few, glorious moments, I believed this man's arms could rescue me from reality. But now? I feel emptier than ever. Any respect I once had for myself is non-existent. I hate myself and I hate my life. I can't live like this one more day. I know what I have to do.

Our son is on a play-date at a neighbour's house. My husband has just come home from work. He grabs a beer from the fridge and plunks himself down at the kitchen table. I sense he's had a hard day. It's about to get harder.

'I have to tell you something.'

'What?'

He stares out the window. *Schlump!* A massive dump of snow has slipped off the roof. An omen?

My heart is pounding. I don't know if I can go through with this. *What will he do? Will he throw me out? Where would I go?* My voice is shaking, barely audible.

'I had an affair.'

His head snaps around, eyes wide, staring.

'It's over,' I add quickly. 'I promise. I'm so sorry. I hate myself for it.'

His eyes close as he turns his head back to the window as if he can't bear to look at me. I'm scared to say anything more but I hear myself blurt out,

'I've just been so lonely. It's no excuse, I know. And I'm not saying it's your fault. I should have told you how I've been feeling.'

Without a word, he gets up from the table. His foot snags on the chair leg as he flings it across the room. Terrified, my breath catches in my chest.

'Don't say anything else. I don't want to hear it. Just shut the hell up.' That was the last thing he said.

Until tonight. The house is dark and deathly still. We're in bed. My heart is racing. He reaches over to touch me. *So soon? Please no!* But I respond because I'm afraid of hurting him more than I already have.

Does this mean he has forgiven me? Surely not.

Suddenly, his hands are around my neck as he hiss-spits, 'Take *this*, you disgusting whore!'

Oh God. Is he going to kill me? This isn't an act of love. This is rage. My mind is screaming…

PLEASE STOP!!!

Finally, his hands loosen their grip. He falls off me and, without a word, rolls over to face the wall. I'm gasping, trembling. *What just happened?* I have never felt more alone than I do at this moment. But isn't this what I deserve?

The "whore" cries herself to sleep.

A week has dragged by at a torturous crawl. Neither of us have spoken. Guilt and betrayal weigh heavy in the air. *How long can we live like this?*

I am not new to suicidal thoughts. I struggled with them throughout the better part of my teenage years. But this time is different. I have no one to turn to, no way out. I'm too ashamed to tell my friends. I can't go to anyone in my church. *What would they think of me?* I don't need more judgement – I have already condemned myself… *SINNER! HYPOCRITE! FAKE!!!*

Heartsick, twisted in a foetal coil, I agonise over how I will end this. I'm convinced my family will be better off without me –

that I don't deserve them – that I've ruined everything – that I'm better off dead.

There's a knock at the door.

My heart is thumping in my chest. I'm confused as we so rarely have visitors. *Why now?* I suck in my breath, hoping they'll go away – hoping they can't hear me.

Another knock. This time, louder.

Reluctantly, I wipe my eyes and open the door, but only a sliver. It's the pastor of my church. *What does he want?* His eyebrows furrowed. He looks worried. Embarrassed, I open the door a little wider. *I must look awful!* Not knowing what else to do, I invite him in. I offer to make him a cup of coffee, but he politely declines.

'I imagine you're wondering why I'm here.' I shrug and look down at my mascara-smeared hands.

'While I was praying today, God told me to come see you.'

Stunned, I have no idea what to say, so I say nothing. The kindness in his eyes unhinges me. Once again, I stare down at my hands. I try to stop crying but I can't.

'Please tell me what's going on. Let me help you.'

What will he think of me? Do I even care? I have no pride left so what do I have to lose? I decide to tell him everything. After an awkward silence, I look up at him – this man I barely know.

Is that compassion I see in his eyes?

'It took courage for you to come to your husband with this. It could not have been easy. But there is something you need to know. God has already forgiven you. You just need to forgive yourself.'

No sermon. No condemnation. No, *Sinner, Repent!* I don't know what I expected, but it wasn't this.

'I would like to pray for you. Is that okay?' Still unable to find my voice, I nod. He bows his head. 'Father, please help my friend. Let her know that you have forgiven her and you love her. Help her to forgive herself.'

He invites me to pray, too, but I don't know if I can. I feel dirty – undeserving. But I'm desperate to make things right – to be a better person. I choke back tears as I open my mouth. I hear a strange sound – guttural – inhuman, as if years of self-loathing and regret are spewing from my lips. My body convulses as I weep uncontrollably.

And then it's over – abruptly – as if someone switched off a light. I sense something's changed. I let a sigh escape as a comforting warmth blankets my body. The shame I felt, just moments before, has left me. *But how? Am I actually smiling?* It seems impossible, but the hows and whys don't seem to matter.

My pastor and I chat a while longer before he gets up to leave. He tells me to call him anytime I need to talk. He assures me I'm not alone. And, for the first time in a long time, I don't *feel* alone.

An hour later, I see our brown Suburban pull into the driveway. A gust of snow catapults my husband through the front door. I shudder from the cold (or is it fear?). Taking off his parka and snow boots, puddles form around them as he sits down at the kitchen table in jaw-taut silence. He chugs down his beer, stares at me, and finally breaks his week-long vigil of silence.

'You will never do that to me again. *Ever!* Promise me.'

'I promise.' I meant it.

It was never mentioned again; a sealed-shut-secret crammed inside a twenty-year time capsule. Until the day the seal was broken – a day I could never have predicted.

Still feeling lonely in my marriage, I crave affection. So when other men notice me, offer a compliment or a listening ear, I am often tempted to stray. I've come dangerously close, but then I recall that knock on the door and the promise I made all those years ago. Still, I yearn for someone to appreciate my beauty, my worth; those hidden parts of me I keep locked away so they can't be trampled on.

Many times, I've wanted to give up on our marriage, but fear and naivety keep me trapped in denial; *If I just believe hard enough, things will change, right? If I could just be a better wife, if I just pray more, if only he'd come with me to counselling. If only, if only, if only…*

But I have come to realise that faith and magic are not synonymous. I can no longer pretend. I am exhausted trying to sustain the happy-Christian-wife façade I have worked so hard to maintain. Outwardly, my cheery demeanour has everyone fooled but, inwardly, I am a mess. I cry nearly every day. And I am spending more time in bed. Sleep has become a welcome escape.

Sometimes, I drive to the ocean as it brings me some measure of peace. But not today. Today my mind is dark like the storm clouds smothering the evening sky. All I can think about is driving off the cliff into the sea but, instead, I berate myself for lacking the courage. *What if I don't die? What if I end up crippled and in pain?*

Gripping the steering wheel – my face turned upwards to the sky – I start to pray, although I doubt anyone is listening.

'I'm sorry, God, but I can't do this anymore. You have to do something… or I will.'

One week later, *something* happens. I am in the kitchen making lunch. I look up and see my husband standing in the doorway, staring at me. There is an odd look in his eyes – a look I don't recognise.

'What is it?'

Nothing could have prepared me for his answer.

'I think we should separate.'

I clench the knife as his words slice through me and hang heavy in the air like a frozen carcass.

I watch his lips move as he says something else, but someone has turned off the sound. Nausea floods my throat and washes over me as the news begins to sink in – *I… think… we… should… separate…*

This is what I'd prayed for and yet… Can this be happening? The agonised look in my husband's eyes tells me he hasn't come to this decision easily.

For the next three days, we don't speak – there is nothing to say. Shards of fear have lodged themselves in my chest, twisting – writhing, as I try to breathe and make sense of what's happening. Life as I've known it, for twenty-two years, has come to an end.

Sometimes, when I think about those dark days, I wonder how I managed to survive. It was what I'd wanted – needed, but it was painful, nonetheless. For a while, it felt like the end but, in reality, it was just the beginning. Eventually, I was able to rise from the wreckage and create a new life for myself. And, as layers of fear and grief gradually peeled away, I began to remember what happiness felt like. Neither my childhood or my marriage had provided me with a safe place to be myself, or ask for what I needed. But, in time, I learned to speak up, stop pretending, and even open my heart to love again.

More importantly, I learned to love myself.

My ex-husband, though emotionally bankrupt, wasn't a bad man. He was a good provider – a good father. When people ask, I simply tell them, 'He just wasn't good for me – we weren't good for each other.' And no amount of wishing, believing or praying was ever going to change that – or him.

I had finally become my own person; no longer controlled by my own brokenness… or anyone else's.

When I look back on those years, I don't feel sad. If anything, I feel grateful – grateful for the two, remarkable sons we raised together – grateful that we parted amicably – grateful that one of us finally had the courage to end things so we could move toward a happier, healthier future.

Although there were many difficult days in my life, that knock on my door – the compassion shown to me when I needed it most, helped me realise I wasn't fighting my battles alone. And that, in spite of my human frailties, I deserve to be seen, appreciated – loved.

As I am now.

Where Are You From?
by Juliet Coe

The wave of boys around me parts. Behind them, sitting in the corner leaning on the wooden rail of the veranda is another. Knife in hand.

He lifts his head; aware he is the focus of attention. Although he doesn't look much older than thirteen, I feel my body tense, conscious of my bangles hot against my skin. He looks to Felipe, the young man who has recently introduced himself to my boyfriend, Mike, and me. Felipe steps closer. With his movement comes a hint of coconut oil in his hair and the smell of sweat, food on breath. In the stalled fractions of a second it takes for veranda-rail boy's glance to skirt past me at waist height, my mind races back over the last few minutes:

How have I got us into this? I've been so stupid, so naïve.

Mike and I, nineteen years old, meandering through the small city of Suva, Fiji; mid-year in the mid-eighties and mid-afternoon. Jungle green hills, a backdrop to the grey harbour walls, contrast with white-faced hotels; houses in bright colours and shops proclaiming their wares with a quilt of elaborate signs. Hindi film music plays on a nearby radio; it's ubiquitous in this melting-pot island country, where at least half the population are descended from indentured labourers brought from the Indian sub-continent to work the sugarcane plantations. The smell of salt tossed on sea breezes mingles with the aroma of concrete pavements exhaling in hot-house humidity.

We're laughing at the memory of last night, 'Wait 'til we tell everyone back home!' The previous evening we'd been to a nightclub in the city. Fiji Bitters in hand, we danced without care. Until a man approached, leaned close so that his face, shining with sweat, was between ours. He spoke in a – "don't want to shout but got to make myself heard" voice,

'I have been watching you all evening. You are beautiful movers. You dance well together.'

We both laughed, 'Us?' I couldn't look at Mike.

'Yes, in my country …' He was from Japan, travelling like us, backpacking like us, having a night out, just like us. 'Where did you learn?'

"Where did we learn?" The compliment was still making us laugh almost a day later.

Is that when they saw us? When we were laughing, holding hands?

'Shall we go through the market?'

Time is a luxury we have as travellers. The term "traveller" one up on "tourist". Tourists get sunburned with ease, drive cars with yellow plates and dither on the roads in alarm at the horn hooting, bus passing local driving. They come here for a week and are gone without learning much about the Fijian way of life. Or so we always spoke of "them", superior in our "local, lived here for years" status. In Fiji, I think of myself as a local, albeit a European local – a traveller returned to base after an absence of seven years. Last week, I showed Mike the market at Nadi, one I had visited as a child every Saturday morning during the '70s. I grinned at hearing familiar laughter and joyful shouts between one stall holder and another and at the quiet sales pitches from those manning wooden-framed, glass carts with displays of Indian sweets, or brightly coloured bangles.

Today, I hope for the same and envisage mounds of watermelons and pyramids of maize piled on stalls or on mats; lumpy earthen yams next to glossy leaves to be used for the Fijian dish *ro-ro*, made with coconut milk, my favourite. We turn towards Suva's market. Will there be squawks of chickens bound by the feet? Or a wonderful whiff carried on the steam of rotting vegetation as we step over drainage channels? Perhaps stalls selling paper bags of ground spices; others peddling *yaqona* roots reaching out like dried jellyfish tentacles – roots that will be ground, mixed with water to make *cava*, that ceremonial, peppery drink I pretend to like. I have never seen Suva's market.

'Come on, not far, over here I think.'

Or is that when they spotted us? When we began to walk on through the market?

'*Bula*. Hello!' Young men, boys appear around us, smiling, gesturing with hands.

'*Bula, bula*,' Mike and I chime.

Two of the older, taller boys, short-sleeved shirts flapping open over t-shirts, continue, 'How are you today?'

'Very well, *vinaka*.' Thanking them, I ask the same and we talk as we walk, Mike chatting with someone at his side, while I talk with the taller man in the brown shirt beside me.

We were easy targets. T-shirt tans on our arms the result of kiwifruit picking in Motueka, New Zealand. Pale legs from winter months clad in jeans to protect ourselves against the land of the long white cloud's winter as we hitchhiked and tramped across the country. White people living in Fiji have legs bronzed by constant sunshine. Plus, how could you forget, Juliet, no European local would be wandering around the market in the heat of the afternoon by choice.

'Where are you going?'

'You mean right now? Oh, just on our way back to our friend's house. We've been buying ferry tickets.' Jutting my chin to indicate the direction of the ticket office, I tell him that tomorrow we're going to the island of Ovalau.

'Eh, *sa*, you should come with me, I will show you souvenirs, we have plenty here.'

Is this "*sa*" expressing regret we were only passing through the market, or at our moving on the next day? I cannot tell. (*Sa* can be a soft sound expressing regret or sadness or said in a slightly harsher tone to imply, "Really?")

Why didn't alarm bells ring then?

Mike is still talking and, together, the group moves, a fluid amoeba-in-petri-dish type way, to the side, back and forth, as we walk up wooden steps to a covered veranda fronting closed stalls.

'We have the best souvenirs, you will see.'

'Hmm.'

We don't particularly want to buy souvenirs, not with weeks of our stay left. I smile at the boys who accompany the taller few in the group. They look at one another, at the floor.

'My name is Felipe, what is yours?'

'Juliet. He's Mike,' gesturing to my side.

'Where are you from, Juliet?'

No practice is needed and I'm off.

'I lived here until I was twelve before my family moved to Ghana, but Fiji's always felt like home.'

How could I have thought that Fiji is home when I'd been away for so long?

'You lived here, Suva?' Felipe's response is swift.

'No, near Nadi.'

'Ah, okay.' He nods, 'Fiji is home to many people, it is a good place, no?'

'*Io.*' Yes, of course, yes; he understands.

'You worked with the airport?'

No one has ever cared where I lived in Fiji. Now, someone is taking an interest.

'No.'

I tell him of the rural area that was home, and the work Dad did, the school my brothers and I attended.

He hesitates, looks at one of his friends, tilts his head.

'*Io*, my uncle lives near there, near to the river.'

'It's lovely. You can see the hills and…'

I tell him of the charity races Dad founded and helped to run for years, ask if he knows of them.

Felipe's flip-flops clack on the wooden boards as he shifts his weight.

'How are you spelling your name, Juliet?'

'J.U.L.I.E.T.'

Sometimes I might add, "Like Romeo and…" but the inevitable, "So he's your Romeo, is he?" as they look at Mike, is too corny for either of us. I glance towards Mike. He isn't next to me. It's okay, I can see his back, he's in the corner of the veranda about fifteen feet away, surrounded by smiling faces. *I knew he'd like it here.*

Felipe repeats the letters I have spelt before he continues.

'What was your father's name? What is your family name, Juliet …?'

He nods when told, begins to talk again without stopping for breath, standing in front of me as he tells of this uncle who lives on the west side, of his cousins who come to stay in Suva with him sometimes, gesturing with hands to emphasise tales of how they come to find work, and then he stops.

Hands held at waist height rather than the gestures in mid-air of a moment ago.

His tone direct, he speaks so quickly in Fijian I cannot make out the words and a voice behind me says, '*Io.*' Yes.

'Juliet. Watch it. Don't.'

Mike is back. Right beside me. He shakes his head.

Something shifts in my stomach.

'What? You okay?'

'Hey, Juliet. See what we have for you here, your souvenir.'

One of the boys around me coughs, the group parts and moves to the side. Behind them, sitting in the corner leaning on the wooden rail of the veranda is another. Knife in hand.

Not good. Now what?

Veranda-rail boy pushes a long piece of dark wood to the side, a flash of light ricochets off the knife's blade as he turns his wrist. But his glance has passed me, he bows his head, takes another piece of wood, and pushes the knife against it, flicking his wrist at the end of each movement.

'What are you doing?'

He is carving my surname on a mock ceremonial knife, the piece beside him says Juliet in stark white letters against the stained dark wood. Letters spelt out carefully and repeated. Skeletal bones of alphabet.

'We have made these for you,' Felipe says, his voice determined, like an unbending metal rod.

'They've done this to me too.' Mike holds up pieces of wood bearing his name, 'over there. Just now. Pay them.'

He's quiet, doesn't smile.

'Why? I didn't ask for them,' my voice is loud.

Mike's guardian steps closer.

'We cannot sell these anywhere else now. They have your name on, eh? No one else will want them. We will lose money. That is not good.'

'How much did you offer them?'

I look from Mike to the carver who has finished and passes the wooden knives to Felipe.

'Fifty dollars.'

'No way! I'm not paying that! I don't want them.'

'Juliet, please. Let's go. Pay them.'

'For you, only thirty dollars. You have a brother? Sister? Back in your country? Give these to them.'

The knives are pushed at me, pale lettering insulting my stupidity. my naivete. **My** *country?* **This** *is my…*

I look through the gaps in between the shifting boys, over their heads, see beyond the veranda. The younger boys have moved further away; one or two slip down the steps and stop, look back at me. *Should I shout? Use the few Fijian insults I know?*

'We'll pay.'

Mike touches my arm.

Reaching for my purse, I pull out thirty dollars. Repressing a desire to throw it on the floor, I splay the notes with my fingers.

'Thirty…'

They're gone. Left before I finish,

'… dollars.'

Melted into the shadows.

My jaw hurts. My head hurts.

'They moved us, cornered me over there before I even knew what was happening.'

'Shit!' I repeat the word. 'How? Wouldn't have happened at home.'

By home I mean the western side of the island, not England, but I know I'm trying to soothe my hurt ego, my despairing sense of belonging, my fallen pride. This could have happened anywhere. We have earned our money through waiting tables, teaching and picking fruit. Felipe and his friends have another method.

The following day we show our tickets as we board the ferry. '*Bula, bula*,' the familiar welcome.

'Where are you from?'

'England,' I reply, '… but Fiji feels like home.'

A Grandmother's Grief
by Suzi Bamblett

My daughter is radiant, blooming. And then, out of the blue, her waters break. It happens at a railway station in a grotty public toilet. She's twenty-two weeks pregnant. It's too early.

I scoop her up and drive her to the hospital. A & E is noisy, overflowing with the usual spate of weekend DIY disasters – burns, broken arms, severed fingers. We join the masses to wait.

'If the babies come today,' says the doctor, 'they're not viable.'

When I'm told I'm going to be a Granny, I can't stop smiling. The scan confirms twins and I'm ecstatic. I'd always dreamt of having twins myself – so special, so magical.

I successfully negotiate a three-day working week; my daughter will need lots of help with two babies. I buy needles and wool and start to knit matinee jackets. In my dreams, I glimpse birthdays, first day at school, graduations, weddings...

Thankfully, everything calms down and five days later they send my daughter home.

Her contractions begin again at twenty-three weeks. She's examined and found to be three centimetres dilated, pain coming fast and furious. They explain once more that the babies are not viable. Everything seems hopeless. I suggest we name the boys.

We reason with the doctors, persuade a lady obstetrician to do another scan. She estimates the boys are a good size. Six medics line up to argue while we plead. Finally, the consultant agrees the neonatal team can attend the birth. They administer steroids.

The contractions subside. There's a change of obstetrician. My daughter tells him she can feel the baby's head but he won't examine her as it might speed things up. He prescribes painkillers and antibiotics. If she can only hold on until the morning, the twin specialist will be on duty.

It's peaceful in the hospital chapel. I light two candles. One flickers, almost goes out, until my partner adjusts the wick. I pray to God.

'Lord please save our boys. Give me strength to know when to argue and when to accept, when to stay hopeful and when to give in.' Over and over, I repeat my words.

He listens. Despite all odds, in the morning the boys' heartbeats are strong. My daughter is transferred to the Antenatal Ward and each day feels like a blessing as we approach that twenty-four-week benchmark.

'We're going to send her home,' says the consultant a few days later.

My daughter smiles as she waddles cautiously to the bathroom to freshen up. Moments later I hear a scream. Bursting in, I find her cradling Jacob between her legs. I run for help while her husband stays. Nothing's ready for the little mite, but he's alive.

She is rushed to a Delivery Suite because George may be coming too.

'Stay with Jacob,' she begs me.

There are tears in the doctor's eyes as he examines Jacob and explains he is too small to survive, his veins too fragile for intervention.

'There, there,' I hold you in my arms, 'Granny's got you.'

You're like a little bird, your eyes tightly closed.

I see a tiny flutter of life. 'There,' I say, 'did you see? He moved.'

'It's just a reflex,' says the doctor.

I don't believe him. I stare into your crinkled little face. There it is again, an angel feather tickling your nose, but I say nothing this time. When the doctor leaves the room, I bend over and breathe life into you. Perhaps I can fill your lungs with love? I rock you in my arms. We love you so much, Mummy, Daddy, brother George...'

The doctor comes back wheeling a crib. 'We need to get him to his mum.'

I look at the crib, so sterile and cold. 'Can't I carry him?'

The doctor considers for a moment, then nods. We walk along deserted corridors to the Delivery Suite.

'Here he is,' I say, as I hand you over to Mummy and Daddy.

Forty-five minutes later, Jacob is declared dead. Over the next couple of days, we live through a nightmare. My daughter's umbilical cord and placenta are still in situ but they don't want to do anything that might bring on George. Instead, they try tilting her bed backwards. Every hour she holds on is a bonus.

I go back to the chapel and make deals with God.

"I'll believe in you forever. I'll swap places in a heartbeat. Take my life not his."

On this bright autumnal day, I feel warm sun on my face as I walk London streets on the way to Hamleys. Why is the sun shining? Selecting a teddy bear for a dead baby is so wrong. I choose a cute cream teddy to accompany Jacob in his coffin and a big blue bear for George to bring us hope.

Four days later the waters around George break. They monitor mum and baby closely. George's heartbeat is strong and he's a good size, but the risk of infection is increased. At eight a.m. they do an internal examination and recommend a natural delivery. A C-section is risky this early in a pregnancy. At nine a.m. they induce the birth.

'Jacob was born easily,' they tell us, 'so George should be quick.'

My daughter's voice is shaky. 'I'm frightened it will happen again.'

'No.' My tummy lurches but my tone is confident, reassuring. 'This is different. George is twenty-four weeks and he's bigger. Everything's going to be okay.'

The labour is difficult; George presents shoulder first. The final stage lasts two hours and, when George arrives, he is born still.

I should have argued for a C-section, but didn't the doctors say a natural delivery would be safer? Why didn't I demand to stay in the delivery room? Could I have said something, done anything to change the outcome? Did I let my daughter down?

Mistakes keep coming. The midwife accidentally pulls the cord from the placenta. After everything that's happened, my daughter must go into theatre to have the placenta removed by epidural. Is there no end? That look in her eyes…

'I'll stay with George,' I tell her.

You're bigger than Jacob. Arms folded, and slightly irritated as if interrupted during a nap. Your towel is blood-stained. My nose crinkles at the metallic smell. I don't want your mummy to see the blood, so I lay you on the bed to re-wrap you. There's a huge gash across the top of your head. What have they done?

'Poor little soldier,' I say, 'you've been through such a battle.' As I lift you up, your head flops backwards and that's when I accept that you've really gone. I wrap you again and cuddle you, telling you how much we all love you.

We're on our own so long I'm sure they've forgotten us. Eventually, a nurse pokes her head around the door to ask if we're okay. The other grandparents don't know yet what's happened, but I can't leave George alone.

The bereavement nurse dresses the boys in doll-sized knitted clothes and lays them in a Moses basket. We give them cuddles, cocoon them with teddies and pictures of our family, take photographs, create prints of hands and feet.

One by one, my son-in-law cradles his dead sons, gently exploring each teeny finger, each tiny toe.

I watch, helpless, mesmerised. How could this happen to us?

My daughter's infection levels are high for another twenty-four hours but by the following afternoon, she's ready to be discharged. Leaving behind the Quiet Room with two butterflies on the door, we emerge from the building, dazed and shell-shocked. We pretend not to notice other new parents, cooing over newborns in brand-new baby seats, while my daughter slips into the back of a black cab, balancing two white cardboard memory boxes on her lap.

Planning the funeral keeps us busy, but things will never be right again. The hardest moment is watching my son-in-law carry that small white coffin into the church. Afterwards, it feels as if there's no point in going on. Jacob and George should be here, growing safely inside their mummy's tummy. Instead, our dreams are shattered.

I had faith in God's power to save our precious little boys. Now I yell at him.

'Where were you hiding? Did you not hear my prayers? Did you not feel our love?'

After a while, I stopped blaming him. After all, if he were the all-loving God others claimed him to be, he'd have acted. I realise now that there's no one listening, and this acknowledgement leaves another gaping wound.

Hope lays bruised, crushed beneath hobnail boots, and I conclude, there is no God.

Tears cascade down my cheeks even when I'm not aware I'm crying. The pain is visceral, it cannot be cauterised. I can't swallow, can't breathe. Just breathe, I tell myself – in, out… in, out… My head is a fog while my heart is made of stone. And yet, in the darkness, something waits. Something still and calm. Perhaps it is love? Unrequited love, crying out to hold my grandsons in my empty arms.

"Bad things don't happen to us." Why do we tell ourselves such lies? When my daughter was a child, I could make things better with a kiss, a cuddle, sweeties or a plaster. To see your child in such pain and know you can't fix it, doubles one's own pain. My daughter struggles to go on without her boys and yet I could not bear to go on without her. I sense she will never be whole again and I grieve, not just the loss of my grandsons, but the simple innocence of my daughter. The light has disappeared from her eyes along with youth and naivety. Experiencing death is the moment one has no choice but to become a grown-up.

With spring comes the news my daughter is pregnant again.

'You must be over the moon,' say my friends.

Not exactly over the moon but quietly optimistic. We're in the best place we can be at this point. For now, this is as good as it gets. Just four months ago we lost our precious boys, and no one can explain why. Twin pregnancies are complicated. I didn't really understand that before. It's early days but we dare to hope. We can't replace Jacob and George. We wouldn't want to. We will always carry them in our hearts. At times I catch myself praying, or at least hoping there may be someone listening. If there is, I ask that this rainbow child is born healthy, to bring comfort to my daughter's empty arms and aching heart.

87

Hardvar to Rishikesh, India
by Sarah Lionheart

December 1987

The next day's bus journey was due to start early so I woke with time to do the exercises for my sciatic-ridden leg. Rattling along in the old bus with the dust and the heat and the noise, I find myself thinking of cold drinks and the longed-for caressing breezes of air-conditioning. Twenty-six years old, a Hindu monastic postulant from England, I appear to be in a very strange situation. Quite a lot of what is happening to me these days is something I do not wish to ponder.

A baby wails, a chicken bundled up above our heads squawks and there is the usual bovine traffic jam as people try to encourage sacred cows to move off the road. The sticky heat is doing more than making me glow. Sweat trickles down my chest and back. The vinyl seat is stuck wetly to my sari. The vibration of the rattles and jolts of the old bus keeps me from falling asleep as does the vibrancy of the scenes unfolding out my window. The intensity of sound and smell is almost too much of an assault on my senses, with loud, bright colours, deafening noise, high decibel conversations in Hindi and bodies packed close with the smell of spicy food, sweet chai and an interestingly mellow body odour overlaid with a musky, metallic smell coming from somewhere near.

After hours of this, we get to the noisy and busy sacred city of Rishikesh. A pilgrimage. I stand. Moisture dribbles down between my legs, spine and breasts. Twisting around, I do my usual scan for any travel detritus that I usually inadvertently leave behind and my God, my seat is a thick wet red. I turn my head to peer at my skirt and there is a growing large dark splodge on the back of my white sari. This redness is pooling on the floor beneath my feet. One of the devotees, a woman, spots my stricken face, follows my gaze and calls out in Hindi to Swamiji, who is leading our group. I am helped off the bus and over onto a low wall where I am to sit and wait.

'We will go and find a place to stay. We'll also get some things that you might need and then come back to get you, okay?' Swamiji calls out to me and off they all go, not quite looking at me. Obviously, I am somewhat of an embarrassment.

So here I am, sitting on a low rubble wall, in a dusty bus arrivals lot, with people gathering around me, excitedly talking and gesticulating, horribly curious. Tears fall into my lap. There is a feeling inside of something in me breaking. My body starts to shiver and the sensation is that I am in a huge underground cavern, dark and alone. There is a howl threatening to escape from my lips so I zip them tightly shut and try to block out the people ogling me. I fix my gaze on my hands time and yet again for the umpteenth time, find myself wondering how it has come to this. This town in northern India appears like a scene in a movie played out before me while I sit with pain splitting my groin. I lift some of my sari pleats to wipe away the tears. No one on this planet that truly cares about me has a clue what a mess I am in and there is not one person here that I trust enough to turn to for help.

Over to my right, there is some movement. An emaciated butterscotch dog comes up to me. He looks me up and down and places his hairy, mucky chin on my left knee. He gazes up at me with eyes so open and loving that I stop crying. 'Thank you, thank you, thank you,' I whisper. Bless him, he stays perfectly still, reassuring me that I am not alone. I love him for it and place my hand on his head.

Thankfully the pointing, staring crowd gets tired and disperses, leaving me with my newfound friend, the two of us sitting there together in the heat. I am dirty, soiled, blood splattered. Not wanting to draw more attention to myself, I look down into the eyes of this stray hound and see they are flecked with brown within the amber. His proud skinny tail wags like a manic metronome to which I am breathing in time, so I deliberately breathe in and out more slowly, glad for this moment of respite.

Now no one pesters me. Now no one comes up begging me to buy food or drinks. Quietness settles. I could stay here, it's a nice place.

Swamiji and three of his devotees walk towards me from the main road. My dog's tail stops wagging and he assesses this new situation. 'We've got company,' I whisper to him. Swamiji's solid large body blocks the sun, casting shadow wantonly.

'I got you a hotel room with a large bath so get up and follow me,' he says. Obediently I stand. My dear dog moves a few feet away, seemingly reluctant to leave me. I wish he would stay.

As I stand, a horn sounds and the light is very bright and my sari feels suspiciously heavy and then my head goes all mushy. What I can see seems to dissolve at the edges. As I slide to the ground, it is like sinking into the softest cotton wool and the most beautiful delicious dark velvet blue blackness takes me into its arms. At last no more pain.

As a little light seeps into my consciousness, I realise I am being carried and people are talking loudly and excitedly in Hindi, gesticulating towards this slight white woman in her white monastic sari in the arms of a huge ochre-orange-clad Guru. It could be a procession. It may be a mob. Apparently, there is so much blood that people are wondering. Even I don't know what is happening: is this an extra heavy period? Is this double extra heavy because of doing the sciatic pain exercises that I was told not to do when menstruating? Or could this be something worse? Something connected to what is being done to me during the night, against my will, by this man whom I thought was going to be my teacher and father figure, those things that I can't bear to think about?

Swamiji smiles and whispers into my ear, 'They think I've done something terrible to you.' I smile back.

It's so nice to be carried, feeling protected, feeling rescued. The hotel is very square and almost municipal. He carries me up to my room where there is a large mottled bath. Somebody shoos everyone out and Swamiji unlayers me. On a chair, there are two flannels, unwrapped long sanitary pads and some brand-new garish towels still in their shrink wrapping. The sanitary pads are bulky, bright and clean smelling. I hold one to my cheek, feeling comforted.

Swamiji gestures towards the chair, 'I sent some of the women devotees to buy whatever you need.'

'I have no clean underwear,' I tell him.

He rattles on the door, shouting hurried Hindi and turns back to tell me that they will go and get a couple of pairs for me.

Normally I would blush to be naked but the part of me that would feel exposed has long been erased by him. I step into the bath clutching the sides with shaking hands. The water turns pink and then a deeper rose. I feel ashamed that I am such a wimp, and that this is so physically difficult for me. As I sit there, the washcloth and soap seem impossibly hard to lift and so he washes my body, pouring buckets of water over me, filling and emptying them several times and eventually taking out the plastic bag that blocks the plughole and letting the water with its red stain drain away. He lifts me out of the bath and wraps me in one of the towels. There is a knock on the door announcing the arrival of some underwear which is white, large, clean and fit for purpose. Together we wriggle them on, place a large pad into the crotch and swap my damp and stained towel for a dry one. I am tucked into a bed. I reach for his hand and thank him for his kindness and care.

I fall asleep dreaming of a wagging tail, gentle amber eyes and the pressure of a slightly scratchy chin on my knee.

It will be decades before I can admit to what happened that day.

Chip off the Old Block
by Chassie Stone

My Dad and I in the near dark, finishing off mowing the lawn and tidying up. The smell of the newly mown grass was earthy and sweet, and I was so happy we were together. It was great having him all to myself and I didn't want to let go.

'See, the stars are starting to come out. Can we lie down on the bank and just look at them, please?' He seemed happy to take a break and lay down beside me.

'What do they all mean?' He had to know, he was a pilot and trained to navigate by the stars, before all the computers and technical gear that are in planes these days.

'Well, always look at the brightest star first and follow the shape and lines to the next one. It's also important to know which month the stars are at and whether it is the North or South Hemisphere.' I thought about it but it didn't make much sense.

They called me a chip off the old block. I was his shadow. Flew with him, and helped him with maintenance on his planes and cars. This was New Zealand in the 1950s. He had his own Ariel top-dressing outfit, the Farmers' Syndicate. Top dressing is another name for fertilising farmland with super-phosphate. He landed his plane in a field opposite our house in Manurewa, fifteen miles south of Auckland. My job was to run across the road to the field and clear the sheep away for him to have a clear landing.

'Come on, help me put the fence around the plane before the cows and sheep start messing with it.'

His base was at Ardmore aerodrome, now an airport, in Papakura. He shared a Nissan hut with a couple of other pilots, one big workspace for them all. Complete with possums hiding up in the rafters. There were about ten Nissan huts dotted about in groups around the airfield, a legacy left by the Americans after World War Two. The best bit though was the concrete runways. I learnt to ride my bike there, pretending I was flying, pedalling furiously along, up and down, crossways. I was an only child and often escaped into my make-believe perfect family fantasy.

He had an old Tiger Moth which he sometimes flew, and didn't think to protect. The cows licked off the *dope* from the wings. The technical term was doped Madapollam – cured glue applied on fine, plain-woven cotton stretched fabric. When he flew off, the material started to unwind and flap in the wind, but he didn't panic.

A daredevil to the end, he taught me to drive when I was ten years old. Out we'd go in the Ford Anglia, to a quiet back road. Change seats and he would put it into gear for me.

'Oh, this is fun,' I would squeal, 'but I can't change the gears.'

He'd put his hand on the gear stick. 'Now, put your foot on the clutch,' and he'd change gears. I could stop, put it into first gear, and steer it. That was about all.

Then, flying, 'Do you want to have a go?' He would put me on his lap and show me the joystick. 'Look at this dial, see the level line? You need to keep the stick steady so that the line doesn't move too much.'

'Will we crash then if I mess up?' He shook his head.

My seat was a piece of wood slotted between his seat and the door of the Cessna cockpit.

My anxious mother asked 'Will she be strapped in?'

Looking at me dad answered, 'Oh yes, a couple of straps to keep her safe.' I had to look away, coughing, stifling a giggle. There were no straps.

'I think you're irresponsible taking her with you, it's so dangerous. As for driving, you better not let her drive alone.'

'We don't mummy,' I butted in. 'I can't even change gears. Dad does it, I just steer,' thinking it would smooth things over.

Life was tricky at home. My mother loathed New Zealand. She likened herself to an exotic orchid, plucked from a beautifully warm climate and thrust into a cold and hostile environment.

They had met in Hong Kong where my dad was demobbed from the RAF after World War II. Kai Tak airport was home to his business as a flying instructor.

Born to American Faith Missionaries in Hong Kong, Mum had enjoyed a cosmopolitan life there before, and after WW2. When mainland China fell to the Communists, a few Hong Kong Chinese and ex-pats prepared to leave. Dad never wanted to return to the UK and announced we would go to New Zealand. The house sold, everything packed up – including a big American Maytag washing machine with an electrical wringer and two Hudson cars – all stored in the hold of a P&O ship, the Chusan.

Dad soon involved himself with an Aero Club at Mangere and applied to be a reservist with the NZRAF.

There was always something simmering in the background, Mum was constantly hyper-sensitive about the neighbours, and people in general. The glances or a deliberate hurtful comment directed at her. "That Chinese woman lucky to get an English man." The label inaccurately fixed on a highly intelligent, well-educated white woman, totally lost in a world of the £10 English immigrants, deriding the Maori as lazy, thieves and layabouts. Suspicious of anybody not from "home."

Arguments when dad came home. All of her pent-up frustrations tumbling out blaming him for bringing us to this forsaken country.

Me, endlessly looking in from the outside, fearful of something bad, trying, oh so hard, in the background, to show them love, to smooth things out.

Then the really bad furious argument. Something I couldn't understand. Shoplifting, police, shame. Slaying him with her words until the sound of a car horn beeping outside. Dad rushing out of the door. A silence followed by her sudden screams and cascade of tears. This was hideous, I wanted to cry but couldn't. Suddenly feeling very shaky I had to sit down, on the floor, as near as I could to her. It was getting very late, and finally, she stopped crying and bent down to hug me and pull me up.

'Don't worry, it will all be alright. Daddy is going to stay over at Ardmore tonight, ready to do a test flight very early tomorrow morning. You go to bed, you've got school tomorrow.'

In the morning she was in the kitchen, making my sandwiches for school. She looked dreadful, shrunken, dishevelled.

'I'll stay home with you, you look ill'.

'No darling you go. I just didn't sleep at all, I had terrible dreams. Like a bad omen.' Her voice shook. I felt so torn, I knew something awful was happening.

My school, Sacred Heart Baradene, was in Remuera on the outskirts of Auckland, 15 miles away, a long journey on two different buses.

Before lunchtime, I was summoned to the Mother Superior's office. As I walked over I thought, what now? I'm sure I've not done anything wrong. I was shown straight into her office and she stood up and came towards me, hands outstretched. My stomach contracted. My eyes never left her face.

She took my hands and held them tightly. 'My dear, you have to go home immediately.'

'Why? what's wrong?'

She shook her head. 'I don't know but you have to go straight home.' I was fourteen years old, left to go back home – alone – a long way, on the buses.

Ninety minutes later, as the bus passed my house, I could see police cars in our driveway. I froze; I didn't want to get off the bus. Walked back from the bus stop, past the Caltex garage and three houses to ours. Walked past the police cars. A huge knot in my throat – a choking feeling. I just knew my daddy was dead.

Connie, my best friend's alcoholic mother, breathing brandy fumes over me, hugging me.

'Come with me, darling, your mother is busy.' she slurred.

Stupid woman. My mother was not "busy"; she was going out of her mind at two insincere, wooden policemen, incapable of giving any sort of explanation. Because they didn't know anything. A friend who was an air accident investigator came in. He told the police to leave and sat down with Mum. I heard him explain to her what little he knew; he was caring and sympathetic and calmed her down. After a couple of hours, everyone left. Dazed, my mother boiled some potatoes, and we ate them with butter. Two sad frightened souls, me and Mum.

She kept saying, 'I should have gone to Ardmore. I could have got a taxi. Why didn't I go? I knew he wasn't right. I should have gone.'

I wandered from room to room, picking up his clothes, sniffing them, and willing him to walk through that door. Now. PLEASE.

Funeral in Papakaura at the parish church. Mum couldn't go, she couldn't face it. Being stared at, the "Chinese" wife. Me, and my best friend Rama, entering the church, hand in hand, everyone staring. Whispering. Being led to the front pew, facing the coffin. I was thinking, *What a joke, he's not in there, he'll walk in, and tell them all to go home.* I started to giggle and so did Rama. Then we both burst into tears.

There was quite a crowd outside the church, with people lining the street to pay their last respects as the cortege went past to the cemetery. We were taken home. Connie was with Mum, both drinking cherry brandy and extremely drunk. They were giggling at each other's silly remarks – totally gone. And Daddy is still not home.

Then the bullying started. The owners of the plane wanted reimbursement for the full price of the aircraft, claiming he had taken it without their permission. The life insurance wouldn't pay out – he was sold the wrong insurance plan. Mum typed letters on her compact Smith Corona, tap, tap, tapping, repeating until she had finished her litany of complaints.

'Read them,' she commanded, as if I knew enough to comment. She was on a mission. The big fight. But bubbling away, just under the surface, a nagging thought. Was it an accident or was it suicide?

'That's your inheritance, the stars,' he would say laughing. 'Think of me when you look up because I'll always be with you'. Sixty years on, I never fail to get excited when I see the stars and knowing I can have my quiet chat with him. Together again beneath the night sky.

Releasing the Narcissist
poem by Peta Heskell

From the shadow of your power,
I stand in my own light.
From the feeling less than you,
I see how small you are.
From the *you are always right*,
I learn to contradict.
From craving your approval,
I now seek out my own.
From fear of not belonging,
I find another tribe.
No leader towering over us,
We're standing side by side.
True friends, we bond together,
No more need for you.

I see you weak and feeble,
Crouching and contracting,
As you cringe beneath the table,
Living in your fear.
I see the smoke and mirrors,
That allowed poor you to hide,
Behind a wall of puffery,
A frightened child inside.
You built a giant fortress,
To protect the less than you,
But when you tear those walls down,
Your fear will crumble too.
The flawless perfect being,
Who made himself so grand.
The fountain of all-knowing,
No one as good as you.

Soon all of your bravado,
Will crumble into dust.
The raw revealing being,
Releasing from all fear,
Will cast aside the fakery,
And open to reality.
Accepting every flaw.
You drop the smoke and mirrors,
Expressing fear
Confessing shame
Releasing anger
Letting go
Sinking down
Rock bottom mud.

Naked to the world now,
You open up your eyes.
A host of loving spirits,
Reach out their hands to you,
'Get up you flawful human',
They lead you up the pathway.
You feel yourself renew.
The arms that wrap around you,
Are holding naked you.
And from that hopeless pit,
Through tears of sheer joy,
You feel the strength inside.
You bow your head,
You take the knee,
They gather close around you.
You sense their tender gaze.
'Welcome to the game,
Humility's my name',
'So glad to have you with us',
Says Vulnerability.

Love takes your hand and turns your head,
'I see your friends are leaving,'
She whispers in your ear.
You watch the distant shadows,
Of Pride and Shame and Fear.
No longer your companions,
You do not need them now.

Welcome to the world,
Time to live your story,
The tale of real you.

No Aid for Women
by Carol Prior

The photo I'm holding shows me as a girl who just turned eighteen. I am posing for the photographer without my glasses, standing half-turned, almost dead centre of the frame, with my left leg slightly bent at the knee, revealing a flared trouser leg that covers the top of my two-toned platform shoe. I think I'm wearing jeans, although they could be "loons" that iconic fashion garment of the seventies. My buttoned-down-the-front short-sleeved mini jumper looks grey, but the almost monochrome photo makes it difficult to tell. It's not my clothes but my face I return to again and again.

I hardly recognise my younger self as she smiles back at me down the years: open, trusting, innocent. How looks can be deceiving – was my hair ever that straight and long and dark brown, almost black? Were my teeth so white and uniform? The back of the photo bears the stamp of the professional photographer: Williams Studios Ltd, and further down, fading slightly, the date – 3 FEB 1973. And it all comes rushing back to me. I was still at school, in the last year of sixth form – but I had left home a few months earlier, in December, just before Christmas. I was applying for Drama School, the Bristol Old Vic Theatre School no less, and this photo would help me clinch not just one audition but two. I didn't get in, but I did become an actress.

It's not the sight of my slim, raven-haired self, without glasses and so impossibly young-looking that causes my heart to lurch, but rather the raggedy lines that crisscross my image on the surface of the paper, badly torn in several places. This photo, like its subject, wasn't meant to survive.

My father was not a man to be crossed. He got his name in the local paper for having a knife in his pocket at the pub where he drank on Saturday afternoons. He didn't use it; apparently, he just needed to prove a point and got off lightly with a caution. And then there was the time he did use it.

One evening at home, after a long drinking session, he started throwing that knife at the living room door, where the remains of his dinner were splattered and lay congealing in brown streaks against the white gloss paint. Laughing maniacally, he strutted around in his gravy-stained vest and trousers, his belt unbuckled, swaying dangerously from foot to foot, not caring about the spectacle he was making of himself and enjoying the fear he saw reflected in the terrified eyes of his wife and children. He was in a particularly belligerent mood, and his pale blue eyes glinted with menace as he took aim and threw the meat knife at the door once more. This time it stuck firmly in the wood of the door, which was already badly splintered from previous aborted attempts.

'And that's what happens when you mess with Johnny Prior,' he roared, punching the air with his fist and scanning the room for approval.

'Come on, boys, up to bed,' my mother said.

It was an early evening in summer and still light outside, but they followed her up the stairs, the dark pupils of their eyes dilated in fear, cowed and obedient. I was desperate to join them, wishing I was four years old like them but I knew that my father was spoiling for a fight and needed an audience.

'Joyce, you cunt,' he yelled, 'get down here!'

'I'm just putting the boys to bed, Johnny; I'll be down in a minute.'

He staggered into the hallway and lurched up the staircase with heavy thuds. Suddenly there was a loud crash in the hall followed by a stream of swear words we were inured to hearing. He had fallen and lay cursing in a crumpled heap at the foot of the stairs. He called for my mother again, his anger now turning to rage. Cowering in the living room with my brother and sisters, my churning stomach growled noisily like a trapped wild animal. I attempted to quell the feelings of terror slowly taking hold of me, the familiar sour taste of bile rising in my mouth that presaged the violence to come.

'Joyce, you heard me, get down here now, or am I gonna have to come up there?'

'I'm coming Johnny,' my mother's voice is quiet, placatory, but fails to mask her mounting panic.

In the living room, we children huddled closer together.

'No, Johnny, please, put the knife down.'

There was a flurry of movement, a scream from my mother, followed by an ominous silence, and it was all over in a couple of seconds. Out in the hall, I heard my father fall to the floor again, mumbling incoherently, his anger spent. My mother stood on the staircase, not saying a word, on her right calf a gaping wound where the knife had sliced the flesh, now pulpy like an overripe tomato.

I don't remember how we got to the hospital – we had no phone – but my mother was patched up, no questions asked. The doctor swallowed her story of falling on something sharp. This was the early 1970s and Erin Pizzey was yet to set up the first Women's Aid Refuge in Chiswick. In the taxi, on the way home in the early morning light, I glanced at my father, who by now had completely sobered up. I knew that something shifted for me that evening. We had endured years of his domestic abuse, which was growing worse with every year that went by. I hated him and was scared that one day someone would die. I resolved to make sure that would not be me.

False Arrest
by Lindsay Tunstall

There's an underlying tension in the village – the stress of providing for *Eid al-Fitr* or *Koriteh*, as it's called in The Gambia, the two-day feast to mark the end of Ramadan. People on the edge of poverty, or over the edge, struggle to buy a sheep or a goat to slaughter. Then they need to pay for traditional garments for the feast day, and all the children must have western clothes for the following day, new jeans, tee shirts, and trainers. The tailors are busy all hours, hoping against hope that there won't be any power cuts to stop them from sewing. Those with treadle machines work on by candlelight. Those who rely on the intermittent electricity supply that blights so many businesses are in trouble.

It's like Christmas; people are determined to enjoy themselves. It's an opportunity to dress up, eat well, and forget your problems. The unfortunate animal is slaughtered, butchered, and cooked by lunchtime. The next day there's a queue at the Health Centre for over-eaters with stomach pains and diarrhoea.

Four days now until the end of Ramadan. It's the rainy season. People are farming, working without eating between sunrise and sunset, and not even drinking water. There's an epidemic of headaches, bad breath, bad temper and road accidents. I know people suffering from severe toothache who won't take a painkiller until after sunset. I admire their dedication, it's not easy.

I am on the compound with German Idi clearing up and doing the chores. I take the rubbish up to the old well at the edge of the bushy area I left for wildlife. Monkeys, enormous five-foot monitor lizards, python and mongooses have a haven there, their last refuge in the village – my mini wildlife sanctuary. As I throw the contents of my bucket down the well, I see legs, naked human legs, just legs sticking out from under a heavy canopy of green creeper in the bush. Oh Lord, what the hell! Give me a break; my brain spins into overdrive. Who? What? Why?

'What are you doing? Come out; *beli*, it's not safe deh! Snakes are there!'

I shout at the legs in the Gambi-English I hardly notice I often speak now. I'm a sponge; I'm always doing it… "Me, I am going to market." Listening to the BBC World Service on my tiny Chinese transistor radio and hearing my native language spoken correctly is strangely soothing sometimes.

There's no response, so I find a stick and tentatively poke the legs, but nothing, no movement. Do I have a body in the bush? If they had to crawl in and die, couldn't they have done it ten feet away from my property?

I go to find Idi, who is making breakfast; lucky us, we could eat breakfast, although I always ate and drank unobtrusively during Ramadan. I didn't want to make it any harder for anyone.

'Idi, come and look. We've got a body in the bush. It's not moving. I can only see the legs.'

'You're very calm, Lou,' he says.

'What did you think? I'd be screaming!'

We rush up from the beach house kitchen, and Idi shouts and pokes the legs but still, no movement, corpse-like the legs lie there. Now what?

'I'd better call the police, I guess.'

I ring Barra police station and explain.

'I'm sorry to say, but I think there's a dead body on my compound, it's not moving, and I don't want to touch it in case I disturb any evidence.'

The police at Barra were generally useless. Sorry, but they were. Whenever anyone called with an emergency, they often claimed no vehicle was available, and if it was, there was no "gas-oil," an unsubtle hint that if you wanted them to go somewhere, it was going to cost you. But this time, they arrive quickly in a pickup truck loaded with men. CID, uniformed police, and a photographer. He rapidly snaps several pictures of the legs from different angles. Then one of the CID reaches out and touches the legs.

'It's cold, I'm afraid.'

Oh dear God, this is awful, and who the hell is it? It's a man, that's obvious. Do I know him? My mind is reeling and unravelling. This is ghastly; who needs this shit. What on earth had happened to him? Had he just died, or been killed and stuffed into the bush?

The CID officer cautiously starts to lift the undergrowth, and it becomes instantly apparent that the man is completely naked. Suddenly the "corpse" sits up! We all scream; it's like a bad zombie movie, and we jump back, shocked and relieved simultaneously. I don't know him, he's a stranger to me, but they do.

'He's from Barra,' they tell us, *'Dafa dof'* (a madman). So many people here wandering about with untreated mental health issues; people say there are more in Barra than in any other area of The Gambia.

They ask if I can find some clothes for him, and I fetch some old trousers and a T-shirt from Maham's house. They hurriedly dress him while I look the other way. Not that he cares, he seems to be oblivious to us all, in his own tragic world.

'I'm sorry you had to come up here, but I'm so glad he's okay,' I say.

'Hey, us too,' says the CID officer, with a shaky laugh.

They bundle him onto the back of the pickup, wave goodbye, and drive off down the beach, scattering the vultures who are picking at the remains of a dead dog.

'Boy, too much excitement for a morning in Paradise; let's have breakfast,' I look at Idi, and he nods enthusiastically.

I sit on the front step of the beach house with my bread and coffee, watching the local fishermen gathering by the river, the same river through which creaking slave ships, packed to the gunnels with human cargo, made their way to the Atlantic. The old trees on the compound were witness to that brutality, the pain and suffering inflicted by humans upon humans. I sense it often, the rawness of it, and I feel the collective guilt of my ancestors.

I am surprised when I see the police car speeding back up the beach towards us. Pulling up in front of me, two officers jump out and look agitated and slightly embarrassed.

'You have to come with us right now,' one of them says rather briskly. 'You are ordered to file a report about this morning.'

'Oh, OK,' I say. 'No problem, but I'll tell you what; let me finish my breakfast and shower, and I'll come down soon.'

'No!' Their voices are becoming louder and more insistent, 'You must come now; the OC ordered it!'

'I'm in my work clothes, and I'm dirty from digging the garden, so like it or not, you'll have to wait while I shower and change.'

'Alright, but be quick,' they grudgingly consent.

Something isn't right. No one had said anything about filing a report. I am suspicious, but when I'm ready, I climb into the truck, and we set off.

'What's going on, guys?' I ask them. I'm curious and slightly alarmed.

'You are under arrest for giving false information to a police officer.'

Giving false information to the police is a favourite ploy to intimidate people, and some languish in prison for years as a result.

'You're kidding me… right?'

'No, it's a serious offence. You are in big trouble.'

Dodgy Barra Police Station. A law of its own. Bribery, corruption, miscarriages of justice, beatings, and torture are the norm. Bribery will flourish when pay is so low that it doesn't adequately cover your family's needs. It's how they survive. Corruption isn't confined to so-called developing countries, it happens everywhere, but as someone here said to me, "In the West corruption is under the table, here it's served up in plain sight."

Barra Police Station is a shabby, dilapidated old building near the ferry terminal. It has a veranda where assorted plain clothes and uniformed officers lounge on benches watching people coming off the ferry, ready to pounce if they suspect drugs, marijuana usually – which many of them smoke themselves – or if they're bored and just feel like harassing someone for the hell of it. At the back of the main building is a walled courtyard with offices around it for Immigration, CID and Drug Enforcement. More lounging. Lots of chatting and flirting with girls who come through the back gate to sell food.

Sometimes, when things are quiet at night, some officers will go out and round up a few sex workers and bring them back for questioning. For questioning? Oh no! They will tell them it's jail or sex. What choice does a girl have?

When we arrive, I am ushered behind the dusty, cluttered front desk, manned by three surly uniformed young men and a woman who stare at me with chilly, censorious eyes.

An officer I don't know looks me up and down, unsmiling and unfriendly and indicates a small battered table in the corner.

'Sit here; I'm going to take your statement,' he says, with a particular menace to his voice.

Eight dishevelled, unkempt prisoners watch proceedings with enormous interest from behind scabby, peeling green bars at the front of the squalid, airless, mosquito-ridden holding cells where they are locked at night. Their conditions are appalling; they were suffering and at the mercy of friends or relatives to bring them food. This must be, at least, some light relief since their incarceration – something they never imagined – a *toubab* arrest!

Westerners are often referred to as *toubab*. One explanation is that it's from the 'two bob' people were paid for work in colonial times. Children often call out as you pass, "Toubab, toubab, gif me minty (sweets), gif me dalasi (money)." Although recently, I have been asked, "Toubab gif me mobile!" Sign of the times.

I've been here for a few years now, and before, I would have been scared and intimidated by my arrest, but now I know how things go and how utterly ridiculous their charge is. What on earth is going on? Oh, OK, I get it, I think to myself. End of Ramadan, everyone needs money for Eid, arrest her, and she'll pay a huge bribe to get out, and everyone will get a share. For sure, that's it.

I sit calmly, smiling to myself at the transparency of their plan.

'Name, address, age?' The officer starts to fill out the charge sheet, struggling to spell the words.

It reminds me of a corruption case I read about in a local newspaper involving the Officer Commanding a police station in

Kombo on the other side of the river and his partner in crime, the ex-Director General of Police. The prosecutor had asked the OC, "Is this the statement you gave on your arrest?" He had stared at the paper in front of him, perplexed until he'd admitted, "I don't know. I can't read." Nepotism rules; it's all a case of who you know, not what you know.

'I want to make a phone call,' I say.

'You can't,' my interrogator replies.

'Your British law still allows me to make a phone call.' I remind him.

The prisoners press their faces to the bars as they chuckle among themselves; this was probably better than a drama on local TV. I pull out my little Nokia and call Maham, who had crossed the river to Banjul earlier that morning.

'Maham, come to the police station. I'm there; they arrested me.'

'Boy, Lou, the ferry is about to reach Barra; I'm coming!'

The policeman tries to grab my phone, so I sit on it.

'Please carry on,' I tell him. He's starting to look somewhat flustered and unsure.

'Say what happened,' he demands, struggling to regain his authority. I recount the finding of the legs, our attempts to rouse the person attached to them, and my subsequent call to the police station.

'What did you say when you called?'

'Well, sir, I said I thought there might be a body on the compound. Write that down, please. I thought there might be. You will notice I didn't say there was a body. As a good citizen, I decided I should leave it to the police to determine what had happened. You know this is going to look very silly in court!'

He opens his eyes wide and looks at me in something approaching horror. His mouth goes slack.

'You want to go to court?'

'Oh indeed,' I tell him, 'Definitely. Please carry on.'

Now he begins to look super edgy. None of this is going according to plan. I should have been trying to strike a deal by now.

When Maham appears at the front desk, I stand up and quickly pass him my phone before they can stop me.

'Maham, find Mr Sanneh's number and call him and tell him what's going on, please.'

Mr Sanneh is the Minister of Basic Education. I had worked with him and his department for the only Special Needs School in the country, raising funding for teacher exchanges to Scotland and equipment to care for these somewhat neglected and marginalised children.

Maham reappears, 'I spoke to Mr Sanneh. He said to tell you, don't give them any butut!' (A small Gambian coin, no longer in circulation.)

A few minutes later, the phone on the front desk rings, and one of the indolent-looking staff picks it up. The officer suddenly straightens up as he's talking.

'Yes, sir, I'm calling for him, sir,' indicating to my interrogator the call is for him.

He jumps up nervously and takes the phone. His eyes stare blankly at the wall, his mouth twitching as he answers, 'Yes sir, right away sir, very sorry sir,' he stutters, standing to attention.

He sits down, visibly shaken. The prisoners are all agog; an excited buzz comes from them. Now what?

'Lou, please go. You are free to go. Forgive me. It wasn't me. The OC ordered it.'

But now I am going to have fun and play to my audience. I smile at the prisoners and wink.

'Really? Go,' I mock, 'First come and now go?'

The prisoners are laughing raucously.

'Yes, yes, you are free. I am very sorry, Lou, please go.'

'What about my statement?' I say, indicating his half-filled report.

He tears it in half, rips it again for emphasis, and tosses it in the bin with a grand gesture.

Toubab 1 Barra Police 0

The Earth Sings
poem by Stephanie Peart

I wrote this poem on the third anniversary of my daughter's death.

The Earth Sings

The daisy sleeps

spider's thread

shimmering in early light

sun-rise in moon sky

a thousand dew-drops

rest on every blade of green

Oh fertile earth!

I see the cream cascade

of hawthorn

I see the blue forget-me-not

and I remember, I remember

Your skin, your hands, your life

everything I ever knew about you

there is anguish in my breast

my heart swells with grief

I am inconsolable.

Sweet Justice
by Peta Heskell

London – 1984

Howard is struggling to heap a mountain of Beluga caviar onto a tiny blini when the pile of shiny black beads splats onto the white linen tablecloth. Cue secret smile. Before he can snap his chubby fingers, the waiter is on it. Scraping the mess into a small silver dustpan, he dabs the offending spot with a damp towel and covers it with a fresh napkin.

'Will there be anything else, Mr Levy, sir?' he asks, with a slight incline of his head as he pours the last drop of Roederer Cristal into Samantha's glass.

'More caviar, and while you're at it, bring us another bottle of Cristal.' Howard waves him away, renewing his assault on the Beluga. Howard isn't big on pleases and thank-yous. This time, the blini stacked with caviar and creme fraiche makes it into his mouth, just. A line of cream dribbles from his lips as he sucks his fingers clean. I'll bet those waiters are sniggering behind his back, but they'll be all smiles and bows when Howard peels off a twenty-pound tip from a fat wad of cash. In Howard Levy's world money trumps manners.

My current squeeze, Simon, and I are here to celebrate Howard's engagement to Samantha and, I assume, to admire the whopping four-karat pear-shaped rock on her ring finger. I guess the Hatton Garden gold business is thriving. The mansion flat in upmarket Hampstead must've cost a pretty packet and Samantha's long blond locks and enhanced boobs make her the perfect trophy girlfriend.

They weren't my choice of friends – they came with Simon. I'd been dating him for a year after meeting at a ritzy party in Bayswater where they served only champagne and white spirits to protect the lush cream carpeting. He isn't my usual type (scruffy, long blond hair or dark and sultry like Elvis) – he's bald. I'm thirty-two. I don't do bald men, or didn't until I met him. The shaved effect, looks kind of cool. And, he's a snappy dresser. Tonight, biker boots, a white collarless silk shirt and a silver-trimmed black suit complement his wiry, muscular frame. Simon's fun, charismatic and he comes with benefits that far outweigh any lack of hair.

There Samantha goes again, tilting her ring finger every time she brings the glass to her mouth, like an uppity-muck lady doing the royal pinky curl while sipping from a china teacup.

'That's some way out rock, girl.' I get a secret kick out of egging her on.

Right on cue, she spreads her fingers and looks down at the ring before stroking Howard's arm.

'He's so generous, aren't you, my lion.' Lion? Cringesville. Is it his thick, wavy, grey hair that reminds her of a lion's mane? I can't and don't want to imagine it's his prowess in bed. Definitely not his middle-aged jelly-belly that smacks more of a hippo than a lean lion. It must be his cologne – Eau de Padded Wallet. I guess it beats working on the cosmetic counter at Selfridges. With Howard footing the bills, Samantha doesn't have to lift a finger other than to hail a taxi to Harrods and... to show off her rock.

'She's a gem, aren't you, princess.' Howard squeezes her shoulder, eyes wandering for an instant to the generous cleavage spilling out of her peach silk blouse before he turns back to Simon. 'Lester gave me a blinding deal on that rock.'

'I love how Cristal matches my colours,' Samantha holds up her glass before draining the peachy golden bubbles. Pushing back the chair, she grabs her cream patent YSL clutch bag.

'Let's go to the Ladies,' she says to me, with a double finger tap to her nose. I know what that means. We're going to powder our noses – but not with Clinique.

The polished oak door with its gold-lettered *Ladies Powder Room* opens onto a plush, wood-panelled salon; the air thick with an indefinable waft of expensive perfumes. Individual dressing tables are dotted with velvet tissue holders, Roger Gallet spray cologne and hand cream. (Today that would be a classic Instagram moment – hashtag poshlooplus.)

Samantha opens the door to a roomy cubicle housing a shell-shaped, gold-tapped sink and a toilet built into wall-to-wall dark wood. A pile of folded white hand towels and wrapped mini Gallet soaps are set out on a side shelf. Out comes the silver box from Samantha's bag. One by one, she removes the trappings, placing them on the glass shelf above the sink – a thin gold tube, a sterling silver razor blade, and one of four rectangular, white paper packets. Opening the flaps of a packet, she uses the tip of her apricot-varnished acrylic nail to scoop and snort a taster of the white powder.

'Wow! Ace gear.'

'Natch, Simon's given you the uncut stuff – ninety-five percent pure.' The four grams of coke in her purse are Simon's idea of an engagement gift.

She scrapes some powder onto the shelf with the razor blade. Chopping and smoothing, repeating the process until there are four long lines. Placing the gold tube inside her nostril, she hoovers up two lines. The final ritual – dabbing her fingertip on the residue and rubbing it into her gums. Eyes open wide, sparkling, huge grin as the drug seeps through her system.

'Here,' she gives me the tube. The coke tingles inside my nostril; I feel it spiking my bloodstream. Buzz on. We wipe our runny noses with courtesy tissues. A quick check in the mirror for tell-tale white specks on the top lip, equipment packed away, and we're good to go.

'Oh, I nearly forgot,' she says, holding out a two-pack of pills. 'Rohypnol – Thank you, Mother.' One of the perks of being a

GP's receptionist is that Samantha's mother can filch drug samples – marketing gifts from pharma reps. Sometimes, after a night on the white, we need something to help us sleep.

'I can't get over your outfit. It's so lush.' She strokes my voluminous sleeve.

'I know.' I stretch out my arms, letting the sleeves fly open like giant wings. The peacock blue parachute silk unfolds as I twirl, and the dervish-style matching pants sway with movement.

'Where did you get it?'

'My friend Reza. He's got a boutique on King's Road. He designed it himself.' I can't resist a bit of showing off.

'Oh really,' her eyes narrow. 'What's the shop called?'

'Anahita. He named it after the Zoroastrian Goddess of the sacred dance.' I take another twirl.

Every girl-about-town should have a gay man pal, and Reza is mine. We'd met, a couple of years back at Xenon, a Piccadilly nightclub, in the Champagne Bar reserved for VIP clients – rich people like Reza. One of the perks of being the owner's PA was that I got to hang out there too.

Reza and I have Persian ancestry in common, but while my lot are Jews converted to Christian missionaries, his folks are Iranian-American elites. The red Porsche and the family-owned apartment he shares with his sister in the heart of Chelsea scream big money.

Reza only had enough peacock-blue dyed parachute silk to make four outfits. I was the first taker at a generous mate's discount. The other two were snapped up in a week, and he kept the fourth for himself. It's flamboyant, like me, and a major plus – it's virtually unique.

Simon's got his cocky grin on when we sit back down at the table.

'Is my gear the best or what?'

Yep, it sure is. Simon's built up a super-profitable side hustle as a purveyor of white powder to the film biz. His day job, picking up and delivering props to and from TV and film sets, gives him first- hand access to people who work hard, earn big and play fast with coke as their drug of choice. At minimally cut, eighty percent· pure, Simon's peddling the Dom Perignon of cocaine, which appeals to my wealthy contacts from Xenon and the Greek restaurant I ran with my ex in Bayswater in the Seventies.

Simon and I are riding high on the shoulders of even higher flyers. Hugo the merchant banker and his partner are weekend coke-heads who regularly insist we join them for lunch at Leonardo's in Chelsea. Plates of lobster or calf liver in sage and garlic butter sit hardly touched, their contents congealing while we guzzle champagne and engage in endless prattle. The lead singer of the hottest punk band places catering size orders which often include an invite to wild music biz parties. Probably best not to mention the royal shenanigans.

Welcome to Thatcher's Britain where Money and Greed swim in the rivers of Excess.

Simon gets up. 'I'm off to the little boy's room,' he says, patting the coke kit in his top pocket. It's more male-practical than Samantha's. The compact, brown glass bottle which easily accommodates two grams of Charlie, has a small plastic spoon attached to the lid – just the right size for a discreet scoop and snort.

Howard leans towards me, beckoning with his finger. A heavy gold chain hangs in front of a nest of shaggy grey hair sprouting from his open pink shirt.

'Got something you might be interested in, girl.' The lowered voice draws me in.

'Wanna make some easy money?'

'Doing what?'

'I'm getting into the loan business. Massive interest every month.' What juicy bait he's dangling – this curious fish swims closer.

'Your cash is lying there, not making any interest. I could get you half that amount again in a year.'

'You're kidding?' The voice that might have whispered to me *"this is too good to be true"* is silent.

'It's a blinder of a deal. With me working your money, you'll get five per cent interest every month, guaranteed.'

The promise of easy money overshadows any moral misgivings. I have six grand stashed at home. I do the maths in my head. If anyone has ever told me *"there's no such thing as a free lunch,"* it hasn't registered. He's reeled me in.

The following Monday I'm in a Hatton Garden coffee bar handing Howard a brown envelope stuffed with fifty-pound notes. After zipping it into his Hermes briefcase he leans forward and gives me a reassuring hand pat.

'You're making a smart move, darling. You'll get your first interest cheque next month.'

If I were a Disney cartoon character, my eyes would be blinking neon dollar signs.

Hailing a taxi, I head for the King's Road in full spending mode. I get out by the Registry Office so I can walk back towards Sloane Square, cruising the shops before hopping on a tube home to Kensington. I'm halfway up the road when I see Reza prancing towards me. Perfect, I was going to pop in and see him, anyway.

'What a coincidence, darling,' he says after our ritual exchange of air kisses. 'Your friend Samantha's in my shop. She wants a suit like yours, you know, the bluebird one.'

'She whaaat?'

'I told her I'd only made four, and they were gone, but she looked so disappointed, and she's your friend, so I offered to sell her mine. I'm off to the flat to pick it up. Come with me.'

'Reza, you don't get it, do you?' I put my hand on his arm. 'I don't want her swanning around in the same outfit as me. It's not on, especially when we hang out in the same places. She's not my friend. Real friends don't do that.' I incline my head, looking up at him with Princess Diana eyes, 'And anyway, it looks better on you.'

'Oooh, the cheeky bitch. I'm sorry, sweetie, I didn't think. No worries. I'll tell her my sister claimed it for herself, or something like that. See you soon.'

Kiss, kiss, kiss. Reza walks back towards the boutique, and I go home, too pissed to shop.

When Simon and I meet up with Howard and Samantha for dinner a week later, she doesn't mention it, and even though I want her to know I foiled her plagiarising scheme, I keep quiet. No point in stirring up trouble. Her actions confirm what I already know – our relationship is all surface glitter with no deep-vein gold of intimate friendship. My triumph has a bitter aftertaste.

It's looking good when, four weeks later, over another sumptuous dinner, Howard hands me a cheque for £300. A Gollum-like sensation swirls in my gut as a *Dire Straits* line runs through my head *"Money for nothing…"*

A slightly disturbing blip when this month's cheque bounces. I call Howard. Not going to panic yet. I'm sure there's a good reason.

'Hey matey, your cheque's done a rubber. What's up?' Keep it light, confident.

'Sorry darling,' he says. 'The fucking bank cocked up. Someone put in a post-dated cheque early, and they let it through. Don't worry. I've got twenty grand coming in a couple of days. It'll be covered. I'll see you right.'

I don't question his story. I don't want to. Of course, he'll sort it. He has to.

When something happens once, it's a random event. Twice piques my interest. But when the third cheque bounces, the pattern is clear. Why does he bother giving me the freaking cheques? He isn't answering my calls, and Simon can't get hold of him either.

The snake coiling around my insides tells me something is seriously wrong.

After two days of being blanked by Howard, Simon calls me. 'Hey, I've just come off the blower with Lester. Guess what – Howard got busted yesterday.'

'Busted? What for?'

'VAT fraud – something to do with gold and, what's more, he's into Lester for twenty grand. Lester is not a happy bunny.'

'Jeez, if he owes that much to Lester with his bunch of heavies, I guess that puts the mockers on me ever getting my money back.'

'Yeah, well, about the money… he never actually loaned out your cash. He's done a Scarface and whacked it all up his nose. At the rate he's gone through it he's probably been *freebasing* (smoking coke distilled into rock – an expensive habit) And the sneaky sod didn't even get it from me.'

I put the phone down and slump into a chair. 'Shit! Shit! Shit!'

On the day of Howard's sentencing, Simon calls from the Old Bailey.

'He got 18 months. The jammy beggar's probably gonna do a sweet stretch in Ford.'

'Fuck him. Ford's a fucking holiday camp. That bastard took me for all my money. They should send him to a prison full of rapists and murderers.'

I conjure up a murky image of Howard in a washed-out grey jumper and fraying joggers. He's trembling in fear of the *shiv in the shower* as he sits on a torn, stained mattress in a dingy, windowless cell with nothing for company but a chamber pot and cockroaches. I'm all fangs and venom.

Anger has been a bitch of a constant companion in the year since Howard ripped me off. His going to jail doesn't make me feel any better, and it sure as heck doesn't replace my six grand. Bitterness bubbles under like a volcano waiting to erupt.

Simon and I aren't dating any more, but we've managed to do the "let's be friends" thing. I'm seeing Richie now whose not long been out after doing a two-year stretch for computer fraud. What is it with me and dangerous men? A rebellion against my parents? An unquenchable quest for adventure? A saviour complex? Maybe. With my help Richie's going straight, working in IT support, but he still has a few interesting contacts.

I try to enlist him in a plot to get the money back.

'How about we get Danny and his guys to jump her outside their flat? It's dark there. No need to hurt her, just put the frighteners on and get her to hand over the rock.' I want my cash back one way or another. My thoughts whirl into a dark hole.

'You're spending way too much time cooking up these fantasies, babe. Don't you see how it's hurting you more than them.' Richie's voice has a soft, soothing quality but I don't want to be soothed.

'I know, I know but they don't deserve to get away with it. They ripped me off. I want my fucking money back.'

'Roll yourself a spliff.' When reason fails, that's Richie's answer to everything. 'Maybe it'll help you chill.'

This Sunday Richie and I are meeting Simon and his new girlfriend for the free-to-good-customers champagne buffet at The Blue Elephant in Fulham.

'Have I got some hot gossip for you…'

Simon pauses to bite into a tempura king prawn, washing it down with a slug of Piper Heidsieck.

'Levy's out, and he's only gone and opened a costume jewellery shop in St Christopher's Place.'

'St Christopher's Place? How the fuck did he manage that?' (St Christopher's Place, off London's main shopping drag, Oxford Street, is a high-end retail area with arty lanes and boutique-style shops.)

'It's not fair, I'm out six grand and he's lording it up in fucking St Christopher's Place.'

'You know Howard, he always manages to slither out of the mud,' Simon sighs. The thought of Howard Levy living the high life ruins my appetite.

I can't help it; I have to see it. I turn into St Christopher's Place, passing by a sushi bar and two boutiques – one selling designer chandeliers, the other eccentric handmade hats. Jeez, have they landed on their feet or what? Their shop sign is art-deco'ish – black with gold and silver lettering. I'm reluctantly impressed. Pushing open the door, I glide in, slowly closing it behind me. No idea what I'm going to say. Howard and Samantha are standing behind the counter – how perfect, they're both here. She's got a few frown lines that weren't there before, and there's a wedding band nestling behind the rock. His belly's bigger, his hair a little whiter, and he looks older than his forty-six years.

'Hi.' I turn on my sweetest smile and, before they can speak, 'What an amazing place! Simon told me you're out. Great to see you again. And by the way, congratulations on getting hitched.'

I babble on, raining niceness until their features soften.

And then I see it.

'Omigod! I love that set.'

The bracelet has four solid rings of black rubber clasped together at intervals by thick chrome bands, and the matching earrings are a long jangle of rubber strips and chrome tubes. Classy punk – the perfect match-in-waiting for my black leather silver-zipped dress.

'Oooh, they're so me. Can I see them please?'

It amuses me to remind him of the word "please"

Howard springs into salesman mode opening the glass case and setting the bracelet and earrings on the counter.

'This is part of a limited edition by a Swiss designer. See those marks…' He touches a chrome bar on the bracelet. 'That's like his hallmark. It's etched on every bar.'

The teeny price labels are almost illegible. Whoa! The earrings are three hundred quid, the bracelet four. What the heck – I put them on and admire myself in the mirror.

'They are you.' Samantha echoes my words.

The cogs whir into place – they are not only me; they are *mine*. I stroll towards the door and open it. A last backward glance reveals them freeze-framed, eyes wide, immobile.

'Thank you,' I say. This time, my smile is genuine. 'I think we're even now, aren't we?'

When I step onto the pavement wearing my new jewellery, they don't follow.

I sashay down Oxford Street, on top of the world. The angry snake has slithered away, leaving a fizzing in my solar plexus, like butterflies flying in formation. Hatred of Howard Levy no longer controls me. Extracting this small but sweet token of justice has released me. The biggest "aha" – Howard didn't rip me off; I was as greedy as him and we both got screwed by our own greed. When that sinks in, I grasp how all those nasty emotional chemicals have been poisoning me from the inside, squeezing the joy out of me. The chorus of Cream's hit song ring in my ears. *I feel free...*

I can't recall anyone ever admiring my cash – "Cute fifty-pound notes, darling." But the jewellery has prompted showers of compliments over the years – "Where did you get that bracelet?" or "Those earrings are wild." Puffing up my chest in a mock boast, I reply with a wink and a smile, 'This is my six grand jewellery.'

Ray of Sunshine Respite Home
by Chassie Stone

I got the job of night work carer at the respite house in May. Doubts assailed me. How stupid of me to put myself forward. I was still grieving for Harry, my late partner, who had died suddenly one week before Christmas. Ongoing worries for my business, my daughter, and my life plagued me. I flitted from sorrow to anger, fear to positivity. Of all the things to choose, was working with terminally ill children the way to go, really? I was still in mourning, wasn't I? There had been one hundred and twenty applicants. I got the job because of my qualification in a Foundation Counselling course, which helped towards the counselling degree included in my employment package.

My hours were 22.30 to 08.30 for four nights a week and three nights off. The salary wasn't great, with no sickness or holiday pay. But hey, it was a charity, and they were paying for my studies.

The focus of the organisation was on whole family care – love and attention for all. I was unsure of myself having to deal with seriously ill children, and it made me question my sanity again and again.

'Hello, I'm Chassie, and this is my first evening. Have you been here before?' I asked the mother, who was cuddling a baby.

Looking at me, she replied rather sourly, 'This is our fourth visit. My husband is upstairs with our sick son. He should be down shortly.'

I ploughed on, 'Oh, that's good, it will be nice to meet them both.'

She didn't bother to answer or look at me. I crept out of the sitting room into the office and sighed. I could see this was going to be very, very difficult. On subsequent visits, her initial icy demeanour relaxed, and she was, in fact, a funny and expressive woman. Her son needed extensive treatment, but he pulled through and has done extremely well.

What did a night carer do? At the start of my shift, after a handover from the evening carer, I would check on who was up and about. Most of the families were in their rooms, either asleep or watching television. The house could accommodate two large families, including grandparents at any one time, or three small families, parents and up to two children. I was told by the manager to watch out for signs of distress – raised voices, and crying. That was unnerving. I found myself prowling about, almost stopping to eavesdrop outside their rooms. Sometimes, one of the parents would come downstairs to watch TV or read, away from their family. The kitchen was a place for confidences. I found if I continued with my work, sorting the laundry and cleaning up the kitchen, the guests opened up. A cuppa, a seat at the table for them, me at the ironing board, steam coming out of the iron, it was a calming neutral space for them to share their fears.

Until I started working there, I never knew much about leukaemia and how many children suffered from the disease. I was utterly astounded and angry that this invasive, cruel disease affected so many people, especially innocent children. There's always a chance of a cure but there are no guarantees. The long drawn-out hope and despair brought back all my memories of my mother suffering from motor neurone disease and of my helplessness in a situation beyond my control. The huge difference though was that I had no one to talk to, no help apart from the occasional advice from the doctor. My empathy for these families was intense. All of us at that house felt the same.

Alex and his parents came to stay as he was approaching the final stages of Batten Disease.

Batten disease is the common name for a broad class of rare, fatal, inherited disorders of the nervous system also known as neuronal ceroid lipofuscinoses, or NCLs. In these diseases, a defect in a specific gene triggers a cascade of problems that interfere with a cell's ability to recycle certain molecules. Most forms of Batten disease/NCLs usually begin during childhood. Over time, affected children may suffer from worsening seizures and progressive loss of language, intellectual abilities (dementia), and motor skills. Eventually, children with Batten disease become blind, wheelchair-bound or bedridden, unable to communicate and lose all cognitive functions. There is currently no cure for these disorders.

Alex was fifteen years old. It was debatable if he would live to see his sixteenth birthday. He loved the movie Ghostbusters and wanted to watch the video over & over again. He would edge down into the sitting room, not yet wheelchair-bound, and ask for the video to be played. He sat there with his arms wrapped around the TV and his face pressed against the screen. Alec was losing his sight and could only see dark shapes and shadows. He knew every line of dialogue and would repeat the words out loud in sync with the movie. That film was his whole world. His parents were wonderful, calm, reassuring and accepting, they had such dignity. That weekend, from Friday night to Sunday morning the video was on non-stop. I was on the outside, remote, self-contained. Did I feel overwhelmed and sad at the situation these people found themselves in? Of course, but I had to put aside my feelings and get on with the job.

Counselling parents was tricky. As a novice, I found I concentrated on too much detail and sometimes lost sight of the main problem. It was absolutely draining. Sometimes it was like opening a tin of worms that cascaded out and then trying to catch them and put them back. When life is normal but a marriage isn't working, parents may reach a stage where they separate and divorce. But when they are faced with their child's severe illness, the instinct is to stay together. However, if underlying problems haven't been addressed, resentment can build up to toxic levels.

Grandparents' anguish was hard to witness.

"Why, oh why couldn't that be me, suffering with a terminal illness instead of my sweet grandchild? There isn't a God, If God is supposed to be full of love and compassion, why is this happening? No, there is definitely no God."

Sixteen year-old Ryan was in the final stages of terminal cancer. The family – mother, father and two brothers – came to stay as often as they could. The charity tried to limit frequent stays for one family to give other families the respite they needed too. But Ryan and his family were just not coping. They loved the home and felt safe and secure when they stayed there. Ryan was already skeletal, his skin, almost translucent, stretched tight against his bones. He was such a gentle soul.

'I love talking to you, Chassie. You understand how I feel about what's happening to me. Do you think there's a life after we die? I hope so. I think so.'

'Yes Ryan,' I'd say, 'I think there is.'

I'd share my thoughts and beliefs, my vision of an afterlife. We had a lot in common. We couldn't talk for long because he got exhausted after about half an hour but I was honoured to spend such valuable time with him and I will never forget him. His parents seemed hurt that I would not reveal any of his confidences.

Ryan's father kept pleading with me. 'Why can't you tell us what you talked about? He's our son. Surely we have a right to know.' This wasn't the first time he'd asked.

'I understand how you feel, I really do, and I sympathise but as his counsellor, I am ethically bound to keep his confidence.'

'If you won't tell us, maybe your manager can persuade you…'

I felt for him. It wasn't about me; he was just a desperate father, feeling powerless.

I looked into his eyes and said softly, 'Of course, it's your choice. If you feel so strongly that I should break my promise to your son, then you have every right to talk to my manager.'

He burst into tears.

'I'm sorry, I'm so sorry.' I handed him a tissue. 'All this waiting and watching, dreading the end… It's too much. It's driving us crazy.'

'It's OK,' I soothed him. 'I know how difficult and painful it must be and how much you love him. I can tell you one thing, though, Ryan knows you are there for him and that you love him deeply.'

Ryan was offered a place at the local hospice, but he was determined to stay at the respite house until the end. The charity was not registered as a hospice so there were a lot of ethical and other questions to debate before they could make a decision. Finally, they gave in and the family were allowed to stay. He was in the downstairs suite of the house.

With a morphine driver in place, Ryan drifted in and out of consciousness. There was no more eating or drinking – I just wet his lips sometimes.

'Chassie, can you set my watch to go off every half hour, please?' he whispered.

'Why would you want to do that, Ryan?' I was curious.

'I want to check that I'm still alive…' I had to hold back those tears again.

During the final days, A Macmillan nurse stayed in the room with him all night, during my shift. At times I was aware of an underlying feeling of fear. Not fear of his death, I'd accepted that.

I think I was scared that he would die on my watch. Yet if he had, I might have been there to hold his hand…

Somehow, despite my fears, I had this feeling that he wouldn't die at night, but in the daytime with the sun streaming into the room. And he did.

After the funeral, Ryan's family and the staff who'd tended him gathered together in a group therapy session to support one another, cry, and share our emotions.

All the families left their mark on me but one in particular stands out for the sheer weight of disasters heaped on them An Italian mother, father, and four little girls aged from three to ten years old. The seven-year-old, Molly, had leukaemia and was in a serious condition. She had been in hospital for some time, had been discharged and they had come to the house for a week's respite. A bright inquisitive soul, Molly loved the playroom and as soon as she woke up, she would rush in there.

'Come and play with me,' she implored, grabbing my hands and pulling me along.

'I can't stay for long, the day staff will be in soon and I have to go home,' I said, pulling a sad face.

She giggled, 'You know how much you love playing with me!' Too true.

Her favourite game was dressing up as a nurse and pretending to treat me, the patient. She'd get the toy syringe out, look at me and say,

'I have to give you an injection, it will make you feel better.'

She pretended to rub my arm before pressing the end of the toy syringe into it telling me,

'It doesn't hurt, it will make you better.'

'Do your injections make you feel better?' I asked.

In a matter-of-fact voice, she replied, 'No.'

I had to hold back my tears; it was as if she was letting me know that she knew nothing was working.

A few months before I met the family, Molly's mother had been hit full-on by a taxi as she drove out of the hospital car park. Her car had crumpled, trapping her inside. It took the fire brigade some time to cut her out of the wreck. They videoed it. She didn't remember anything; even when she saw the video, nothing jogged her memory. She was a mass of broken bones and nearly died from her injuries. When I first saw her, she was still using crutches, after a long spell in hospital. She was slowly gaining enough strength to manage with just one crutch and then none at all. Molly's father's world had come crashing down with this double whammy but he handled it even though he still had to work every day. They were such an upbeat, positive, fighting family.

At an evening handover, Kevin, who worked on the day shift, asked me if I would like to join in with a fundraiser for the charity. They were planning a fun rugby tournament to be held at the Rugby Club. It was a game of mixed touch rugby and people were tasked to put a team together to play.

'Would you like to play or help out on the stalls or pitch?' he asked.

I liked that idea. 'If you're short of players I'll go onto the pitch. I don't know anything about the game, but I'll have a go.'

What a successful day. I joined in a couple of games, running about and filling in for teams that were short a person. I was converted and put together my own team of mixed players – the Beauts and Beasties. We played for a couple of years raising funds for the home.

I worked at Ray of Sunshine for four years and gained my counselling degree. But eventually, it took so much out of me that I had to leave. I was running on empty; emotionally drained, no longer capable of empathy or sympathy, hearing but not listening. It was time to go.

The work was exhausting at times – and I had to study on top of that – but the resilience and hope that I witnessed in those families spurred me on to finish my degree and deepened my resolve to live each day in gratitude.

Staggered by Nicola Field

So there we were: a mum, a dad and two daughters. What else was there to be but a family?

I couldn't get comfortable. The seat was too slippery. I put my foot on the back of mum's seat and pushed myself up.

'Gedahhdervit!' Mum twisted round, her nostrils flared out, her arm swung up, ready, 'Yerrrr… troublemaker!'

That was a shock and I felt cold stuff tip over my insides.

We were all driving home from Saturday shopping in Reading. It was pouring with rain. There was a traffic jam so we just crawled and kept stopping. The windscreen wipers sloshed backwards and forwards: *Eek chooomp! Eek chooomp!* It was too dark to read and The Mystery of Banshee Towers slipped onto the floor.

Pammie's feet only reached the edge of the seat, so she dug in her feet to stop slipping down. She combed her Sindy doll's hair, combed and plaited.

Frank was driving. Men always drive, unless there's something wrong with them. His head and Mum's head were flashed up by sliding lights from other cars. Mum's hair was flat on the back from her headrest and parted on top like a devil's horns. Frank's brown, wispy hair ticked on the top of the car. They were talking about the new bedroom again, in droning voices. Frank talked as though he could hardly be bothered to open his mouth. It made all his words stick together.

Mum said, 'Do the beds go up before the carpets go down?'

Frank said, 'Oooh-slowdownslowdown.'

'Whaddyamean, slow down?'

'Frame-first. Thasswhy-we'restoppingoff-forbrackets. Yousortoutyourcolourscheme.'

'I've sorted it out. Orange with brown. All the rage for children.'

The windows were steamed up. Frank pressed a button and a hum started.

Slipping down, I leant across Pammie and blew on her window to steam it up more and drew with my finger in the fog, a girl in a midi-skirt with pageboy hair. The last bit made a squeak and I saw Frank's eye in the mirror, swivelling about, slimy, and I slithered back to my own side.

'Arethosegirls makingmarksagainCarol?' he muttered.

Mum's face again, mauve lips. 'HOW MANY TIMES DO I HAVE TO TELL YOU?'

'It was her!' Pammie pointed.

'No it wasn't!' I tried and mouthed 'Pig!' at her and made a threatening, pinching sign.

Mum's eyes had eyeliner. 'You'd better watch it, my girl... Your lies won't help you.' I said: 'What's wrong with it anyway? It's a decoration.'

Mum said: 'It stays for days, makes Frank look silly when he goes to British Aerospace. And it obscures visibility.'

'What's that mean?'

'DON'TARGUEWITHMUMMYDOASYOU'RETOLD.' Frank's hair was tickling, tickling and his slimy eyes flicking about. We all jumped, me and Pammie and Mum. 'ABIG NINEYEAROLDGIRL LIKEYOU.'

Mum's face went quieter. 'Just don't do it,' and she turned back to be in the front with him. I let all the other sounds sink down and listened, still as a statue.

'She was only asking me what visibility meant.'

'She was causing trouble. You know the answer, Carol.'

He often said this and I wondered what this answer was. Boarding school, prison, approved school. In The Planet of the Apes, people had operations to take their brains out so they only walked about in single file. He might want to lock me in a room or a wardrobe. That's why I learnt off by heart how the Five Find-outers got away whenever smugglers or gypsies took them prisoner. I hated him. He had no right to tell me what to do.

'DOH A DEER A FEMALE DEER' Pammie sang all of a sudden. It always made everyone sing.

'Shut up!' I shoved her with my fist, not hitting, and felt my teeth clench. It was too late.

'RAY A DROP OF GOLDEN SU-UN!'

Mum and Frank joined in. The air got thick and deafening and lights outside cut in my eyes.

'MI A NAME I CALL MYSELF! FAH A LONG LONG WAY TO RUN!'

It happened earlier in the department store, the thing that made Mum and Frank hate me. They had chosen the carpet for the sitting room and Frank was writing the cheque on the sideboard where you pay. I put my head up on it. I liked the look of the fountain pen, and the ink coming out wet. The shop lady said to me:

'Do you like seeing your Daddy spend his money?' and then she smiled around, expecting everyone to laugh.

Lies are wrong, even when you agree with wrong things it's a lie and deceitful. And I knew God's eyes were watching, watching everything. God was on my side. But I couldn't shout it out: *He's not my dad!* so I told the truth looking down not opening my mouth so it came out as a sound without words.

'Pardon dear?' said the shop lady. 'Pardon?' but I looked up and kept my mouth shut and my face rang and I saw Mummy watching, watching, holding her breath.

And I had done wrong, wrong, wrong. It was wrong to be right.

Then Mummy laughed poshly, shouting, 'Oh I think we'd all like spending other people's money if we had the chance! Ha ha ha!'

And the grown-ups all laughed and when they had finished they walked away and I followed.

At school people always say "My mum and dad this" and "my mum and dad that."

Ladies in the road asked Mum "What does your husband do?" and Mum just said, "He's an engineer."

I went to tea at Julie Ashwin's house and her mummy asked me if my mummy and daddy were enjoying their new house and I said 'He's not my father,' and there was a shock and a silence like after something breaks. She said, 'Is your real daddy dead?' and I said, 'No,' and she said, 'Oh then your mummy has got a new husband,' and I said, 'No, they're living in sin.'

I had to never give in to it. 'Don't ever let him kiss you,' Daddy said. I had sort of kissed him, though, at bedtimes, but I kept my face down and didn't touch his face with my lips. And I found ways to make up for breaking my promise.

Now the car moved forward a bit faster.

'SOH A NEEDLE PULLING THREAD! LAH A NOTE TO FOLLOW SOH!'

Pammie's voice got louder and more excited as it went they were all singing together.

I tried to spoil it, change it and started up: 'I AM SIXTEEN GOING ON SEVENTEEN!'

It didn't work. 'TI I DRINK WITH JAM AND BREAD!'

I tried again, 'I NEED SOMEONE OLDER AND WISER!'

'THAT WILL BRING US BACK TO DOH OH! OH! OH!'

Frank stopped the car to get things to build with and got out walking, running in the rain, he looked like Humpty Dumpty.

We three waited.

'Frank's going to a lot of trouble making these bunk beds for you two, you know,' said Mum.

'I didn't ask him to,' but I said this mouthing downwards.

'They're not like ones your friends will have. They're really modern, staggered. We got the idea from Ideal Home.'

'Mummy,' I said.

She turned around, nearly smiling. 'Yes dear?'

'Don't you love Daddy anymore?'

The rain got brighter. Mum went forward. She jerked up her head and opened her mouth. For a second nothing came out. Then, she said, as if she was on tiptoe, 'I suppose I don't.'

The seats creaked. Pammie started undressing Sindy. The wipers wiped. *Eek chooomp! Eek chooomp!* I looked at the watch Daddy gave me for Christmas. Swiss Chalet. Seventeen jewels. Unbreakable mainspring.

When we got going again Frank kept looking at Mum and he didn't know what was wrong. Good.

'Half past four!' I shouted, 'Doctor Who! We mustn't miss it!'

'What time's it start?' said Frank.

'Five fifteen! Five fifteen! You know! Go faster!'

'I can't break the speed limit dear.'

Don't call me your dear. If I missed Doctor Who, there was nothing left. I jammed my head down on the seat and screwed up my eyes and prayed, mouthing:

Dear God, please don't let me miss Doctor Who. Dear God, please don't let me miss Doctor Who. The seat smelt of Frank.

Please, please, please. I. Beg. Of. You.

I kept praying and looked up out of the back window. It was dark, with stars coming out and then being hidden by huge black clouds. In front, Frank had his hand on Mum's leg. My skin wriggled.

I leant over and nudged Pammie, pointed at Frank's hand, put my hand over my mouth and pretended to giggle. She copied. I went: 'Hee hee!' and she copied again. 'Ha ha ha!' Mum stared ahead and breathed out, loudly. 'Hee hee! Heh heh heh heh!' Finally, Mum said 'Oh I can't stand it,' and pushed Frank's hand off. Good.

Daddy was all alone eating his dinner off a tray.

It was near home now and I put my face up to the window and closed one eye then the other, winking faster and faster. The moon went backwards and forwards over the hill. The window steamed up and I rubbed and zigzagged a hole to see through.

The car jumped on the spot. Frank swung round THWACK!

I screamed.

'Oh god,' Mum moaned.

The sting went bang on the top of my leg and I cried.

'DON'TDRAWONTHEWINDOW! '

'I wasn't!'

'DOYOUWANTANOTHERONE?'

'No! I didn't!'

Pammie was combing, combing.

'Don't fib, Angela,' said Mum.

We drove on. I felt everything coming up in my chest - I hateyou I hateyou I hateyou – and held it in and held it in and when I got out the seat by my head was dark and wet.

When the beds were finished they looked like giant steps stuck on the wall. I was the bees' knees when my friends came to tea. Everyone came upstairs to have a look, auntie and uncle and the people in the road, and the milkman. While they stood and stared, I climbed up and down my ladder. Mum held her breath and kept her eyes wide open and her mouth was happy.

'What a clever man!' they all said.

'What a kind man!'

And my prayer was answered that day because we did get home in time. I ran in and switched on and it warmed up and it was the end of Grandstand, with the camera swinging around a big crowd.

Then: *Daddleadum! Daddleadum! Daddleadum! Daddleadum!*

Eeooooooo! Eeeee! Oooooo! Daa dla da! Daa dla da!

'You're your own worst enemy, Angela,' said Mum, coming in with bags.

'Shhh!' I nearly said, "Shut Up".

Errrk! Errrk! squawked the Tardis.

'Don't tell me to shush!'

'Exterminate! Exterminate!' screeched the Daleks.

A Chance in Hell
by Carol Prior

It's quiet in the classroom. There's only me here and the teacher who's invigilating. A bell rings and rouses me from the frantic scribble of wild calculations covering the Maths exam paper. Home time. The sound of hundreds of teenage girls leaving school on a Friday afternoon in high spirits. I wish I were with them.

I glance at the clock – 3.35 pm. Have I really been here an hour already? I look down at the page in front of me. It's no good; I can't make any sense of the figures. Mr Wallace told me it was okay to show how I had reached an answer, but the page is a mess of hieroglyphs that I have no chance of deciphering. Oh God, I'm going to fail again! Why did I agree to this resit? I want to be an actress, not a mathematician.

It's 3.45 pm. I'm running out of time. Tears well up behind my glasses, blurring my vision. The clamour of caterwauling schoolgirls recedes, replaced with only the sound of my heart beating loudly in my ears. My head aches and my eyes are dry and scratchy from lack of sleep.

Last night I was dragged out of my bed and made to stand in the corner of a cold bedroom while my father, with terrifying and monotonous predictability, brought himself to a climax just inches behind me. Eventually, the nightmare ended, and exhausted and craving the oblivion of sleep, I crawled back to my bed as dawn was breaking to the sounds of milk delivery on the suburban street where I lived.

My palms are sweaty as I swallow hard to quell the mounting panic and attempt to refocus on the page in front of me that's covered in a code I have no chance in hell of cracking. Tears tumble down my cheeks and I remove my glasses, dropping my head into my hands. A feeling of utter desolation sweeps over me. I must have made some sound because the teacher is making her way toward me with an expression of concern on her face.

'Are you alright Carol?'

I shake my head and burst into tears. 'I'm sorry, I can't understand what I've written. It's all gone wrong. I'm going to fail again and let everyone down. Oh God…'

The teacher gives me a tissue, 'If you like, we can take a break for five minutes. You are allowed one five-minute break. Maybe you can go to the toilet and dry your face? You'll feel better.'

In the toilet, I run the cold tap and douse my tear-stained face – all red blotches and puffy eyes. I grab my glasses and clean them on the hem of my shirt. I must hurry. The longer I linger, the less I want to return to the exam room. I'd worked so hard for this exam, sitting night after night in the unheated back room, wearing three jumpers just to keep warm, while World War Three raged around me. Indignation blazed within me. I will NOT let him stop me from passing! I was clever and knew the way out of the hellhole of my childhood was through education – chances he never had and chances I was going to grab with both hands. Putting on my glasses, I face myself in the mirror once more, holding my gaze for a moment to steady myself. I'm calmer now. I step out of the toilet with a new resolve.

I got my Maths GCSE the second time I took it. I don't remember what a quadratic equation is or how to solve it, but without my Maths exam, I would never have got a place at Bristol University to study Drama. I'm so proud of my sixteen-year-old self who overcame incredible odds to give me the life I enjoy today. I owe her everything. And I'm very grateful for the kindness of that teacher, whose name I will never know, at such a pivotal moment in my life.

And you know something else? I did become an actress after all.

My Mother's 35th Birthday
by Sarah Lionheart

Bahau Estate, Malaya; Tuesday 29th Nov 1960

Tony is bringing the car around from the garage and his red cigarette end dances in the gloaming like a drunken firefly. 'Tell the cook we won't need dinner tonight,' he shouts.

My mother turns into the house and relays this to Yu Yan, the Chinese girl who is the *amah*.

Yu Yan lives up to her name with a truly radiant smile. She is holding a nearly one-year-old girl in her arms and feeding the child a banana.

My soon-to-be-mother steps into her smart shoes at the door and stands languidly on the veranda. Around her, there is a delicious thrum of the music of the Malaysian birds and insects, dancing their end of the day. The evening fragrance of flowers, especially polianthes and jasmine, smells divine after a busy, dusty work day driving up and down the local roads to the hill station clinics, checking on maternity care and the many medical social work tasks that shape each day for her.

Here come her Siamese cats, arching and proud, yowling their goodbyes whilst delighted to claim their home for themselves for the evening, free to lounge wherever they desire. My mother's small car is resting in the shade of the coconut tree, a dangerous place to park. She calls the gate boy to move it and wash it before he goes home.

I hope, for that moment, my mother felt happy and blessed standing there, enjoying the beauty of her home and that lush garden before her. I like to think she was able to pause and savour it. However, this is highly likely to be wishful thinking as I only ever saw my mother savour inhaling her cigarette; or, later in life, standing back to admire her flowers. Usually, she gave the impression of keeping going, not looking too closely into how she felt or what she wanted, only eager to be distracted. I regret we never talked openly again after those fireside stories in my early teens.

Sadly, I was probably too much for her. She needed a more straightforward daughter. After the typical years, so many daughters go through, of castigating my mother for all her numerous failings, I have now got the painful wisdom of hindsight and recognise that she was raised by the "momster" of all mothers. Flawed and fragile, she struggled herself to be a good enough mother. Here on this evening, she is in her prime. Today in 2022, I am grateful to her for many things: my Irish passport; her adventurous spirit; her creative flair; her ability to tell a good story; her determined fight to save my life, but all that is in the future. On this night, she is simply a young woman and new mother looking forward to a dinner dance. If I am brutally honest, she probably felt her dress was too tight, the evening too humid, and irritated that her natural curls were sticking damply to her forehead.

Even so, let's for a moment stand here with her. Today is her thirty-fifth birthday (middle-aged if you go by the Bible life span of three score years and ten.) As a birthday treat, they are going to the Colonial Club for a dinner dance, free from baby duties. My not-yet-my-father is just a few months over thirty, but my mother never tells him she was born before him in 1925. Her wedding certificate gives her birth date as 1930, making her four months younger than him. So today, she is thirty by his reckoning. It's a puzzle to me as she always told me that I was born when she was thirty-five, so maybe my dad just isn't good at sums or has learnt not to think too deeply about the details of a lady's age. Knowing my mother, she could not have coped with marrying, at thirty-three, a man who was only twenty-eight.

Before my sister Jane's birth, her first child, a boy was stillborn. And now, only a few months earlier, she had gone to the bathroom and discovered blobs of blood and miscarried a baby boy. My two brothers were lost to me before I was even a twinkle in my mother's eye. I don't tell you for you to care. I tell you because, as you know, this is life. No one's tragedies are mundane, certainly not yours. Nor mine.

On this gloriously perfumed evening, a twinkle was in both her eyes. Then my father pulled up in the car and saw her standing there. With her pale blue Irish eyes, her luscious dark curly hair, flawless skin and the pretty white tight-waisted dress made especially for her by the local tailor, several twinkles waltzed merrily in his eyes too. And it would have been a good evening. They had many friends, and it was normal for them all to meet and socialise at the club. She was always loquacious and entertaining. They would have come home weary but happy – and not so exhausted that the fun could not continue. That was the night I was conceived to the chirrup of insects outside and the whir of the fan generously gifting its cooling breeze to the heavy hot air.

Within a few weeks, my mother was retching over the toilet bowl. It was a good sign; they wanted more children. But this was severe morning sickness, and she was beginning to feel ridiculous, turning up for work with an empty container to catch sudden vomit. The previous miscarriage and the stillbirth had left her fidgeting and nibbling the edges of her nails. She would lie at night watching the ceiling fan and pondering how new life seemed so precarious, so easily taken. Her hands cupped around her belly, wishing to keep "foetus-not-yet-known-as-Sarah" safe. I was oblivious, cradled in my amniotic sac, staying female, growing my spine, limbs and brain, still not developed enough to hear or feel too much. In the early evening, they played with Jane, who was now shuffling around on her bottom. They rubbed floor polish onto her terry cloth nappy, and she hauled herself around the wooden floors, leaving them polished and fragrant.

One morning, my mother didn't quite make the bathroom in time, and the vomit went all over the floor.

'This is more like morning, afternoon, evening and night sickness,' she said with weary humour.

On her work rounds that day, one of the doctors gave her some pills to help. He'd given them to her when she was pregnant before. She only took a couple and then stopped. She placed the package on the passenger seat and threw up again. She was losing weight. ("Always good for a woman," she would say, "but bad for the baby". She was of that generation.)

At dinner that evening, the smell of the meat set her heaving. She staggered from the table and threw up all over her indoor sandals.

"It will make me feel worse to take the pills on an empty stomach," she thought. "I'll wait until I next eat…"

The following evening, the cook thoughtfully made steamed fish, very bland, with plain rice. There was a quiet murmur from the veranda as my parents chatted about their day: the rubber plantation, the clinics. When the gong sounded, they went inside, and she ate the fish. She didn't throw up.

'I'll wait another day,' she said.

The days went by, and she was throwing up a bit less. Four days later, she was six weeks pregnant, and the pills were no longer as urgently needed. Prising the lid off their bottle, she flushed them down the toilet and slipped under her cool cotton bed sheet. The whirring fan lulled her to sleep. The next morning she was only mildly sick and reminded herself that losing a bit of weight wasn't ever a bad thing.

Me? I was cocooned in my sac, my arms and legs growing normally – saved from the effects of Thalidomide.[*]

---

* *Thalidomide was a drug prescribed to pregnant women in the early 1960s to relieve severe morning sickness. As a direct side-effect of the drug, babies were born with horrendous defects – others unable to survive the abnormalities it caused.*

You Said I Said
poem by Micki Findlay

You said
I had no clue how to make a bed.
Who told you to tuck the sheets in that way?

You said
I wasn't doing the laundry right.
Didn't your mother teach you anything?

You said
I didn't keep the house tidy enough.
You call that clean? Watch how I do it!

You said
I couldn't cook like your mother.
She made everything from scratch. Why can't you?

You said
you were angry because I wasn't home.
Where were you? What took you so long?

You said
I couldn't do anything right.

And
when I did everything "right"

You said
nothing at all.

I said
I can't live like this anymore.

I said
I'm tired of crying.

I said
*No matter what I do
it's never good enough.*

I said
I'm fed up with trying.

I said
Oh and by the way

I know how to do the fucking laundry!

And then I said

Goodbye.

Bitter Cold Days
by Delia Louise Seville

March 1969

Strangely, I was grateful for the workplace. It had become a sort of refuge. A few weeks before starting the job, Mrs Dean had thrown me out of her house. She was the mother of my friend Ruth from school, and it seemed like my only option after running away from home. Initially she had insisted I get a job to pay my way. So, I did. I later discovered she'd had several phantom pregnancies after her six children had flown the nest. Maybe this was what led her to take me in.

That morning, I woke up feeling faint and feverish. Hardly able to walk to the bathroom, I had fallen back into bed. Mrs Dean came halfway up the stairs and glared at me through the bannisters.

'Get up and go – get out of my house.'

My throat tightened. My tummy lurched. 'Go where?'

'You're not staying here in bed all day being waited on hand and foot. You can find somewhere else to live – and I mean from tonight.' Her head looked small on her six-foot-tall frame. She had once dreamed of becoming a model.

It was a lonely half-hour bus ride to Aylesbury, the nearest town. On a postcard in a rundown shop window were written the words Room To Let. I scribbled the address on the back of an old bus ticket and asked a stranger for directions. I found the small terraced house down a back street and tentatively knocked on the door. It opened.

'Allo. What-a you want?' said a short, tubby man in a white vest. He had a Mediterranean tan and accent and receding, black, Brylcreemed hair.

'I've come about the room if it's still available please?' I tried to sound mature beyond my years.

'Si, come, I show you.' He looked me up and down and opened the door a little wider.

I clutched my bag to my chest. A strong aroma of garlic hit me and for a moment I felt I might be sick. He led me through a dark narrow hallway and up a flight of stairs covered with a threadbare carpet. He pushed open the door to a back room off the colourless landing. Thin cotton curtains which were too short for the window hung between walls of cracking plaster. It was more like an extended cupboard. It smelt musty. An old, scratched wardrobe fitted alongside a grubby double divan bed, with barely room to walk between. I wanted to run out of the house.

'Here, see? Bring own sheets, share kitchen, and bathroom downstairs. Three pounds ten shillings a month. I Antonio. You-a want it?' He seemed impatient for a reply.

I hoped he could not sense my feeling of desperation.

'I'll take it. My husband will follow soon. He's away working.' I felt my face go red as I looked down at the wooden floorboards.

No heating, no bedding, and no husband. I shivered. Swallowing hard, I went out to a telephone box and rang Mrs Dean. She spoke in her usual abrupt manner.

'Give me the address and Mr Dean will drop off your stuff and the old cot when he comes home.'

I told her, and the line went dead.

Mr Dean, a small skinny man, ruled by his wife, would not be able to refuse. I think he tried hard to stay out of the house as much as possible. Mrs Dean would cook his evening meal at seven in the morning. She plated it, put it in a warming oven, and there it would remain until he walked in at night after a long day at work. I would sit back and pretend I wasn't there, watching as he silently ate dried-up meat with thick congealed gravy and lumpy mashed potato while she complained to him about her soul-less day. She usually found some way to tell him how pathetic he was.

I returned to the new house and waited in the cold bedroom. The faint feeling returned. Eventually, sleep came over me as daylight was fading. The doorbell jolted me out of a dream of beautiful horses galloping through the pure snow and me, carefree, being carried with them, to a land far beyond.

Antonio shouted up the stairs,

'It-a a man for you,' he disappeared out of the front door.

Mr Dean did not come in but simply said one word. 'Sorry.'

There was a look on his face that told me he was not at all surprised that his wife had made me homeless. I felt sorry for him. The brown weathered cot leaned up in pieces in the empty wardrobe. The house was silent. I could not think or feel anymore, only shiver.

Antonio approached me on my second night.

'You want-a to stay in my room tonight? There's heater. My little daughter, she there sleeping, I sleep downstairs. My wife she in Italy, back-a next week.'

In my cold, exhausted, pregnant state I found it hard to refuse. His child asleep on a camp bed made it feel safe enough.

I was drifting off to sleep, snuggled under the bedclothes, in a foetal position facing the wall, when I felt the mattress move. A smell of cheap aftershave, sweaty armpits, and beer wafted across my face. A cold hand grabbed my shoulder from behind. I gasped.

'What are you doing? My husband will not be pleased!'

That was all I could think of to say. I got out of bed and ran barefoot, past the sleeping girl and the paraffin heater, to my freezing room.

I fumbled to twist the key in the door. Then sat on the bare, striped, horsehair mattress, clutching my knees, my heart racing while Antonio banged on the door and kicked it.

'Let-a me in, let-a me in,' his voice got louder, 'let-a me in, you have man in there, I have-a right to search-a the room.'

'That's ridiculous. There's nowhere to hide in here. My husband's back tomorrow,' I said through the tears, trying to sound mature.

'You-a no husband,' his voice escalated and the kicks became like beats on a wooden drum.

Even though he was drunk, there was obviously no fooling him.

After what felt like hours, the shouting and banging stopped, but my tears didn't. The night passed and I remained frozen, unable to sleep. Sunrise made little difference.

All seemed quiet in the house. I tiptoed down the staircase and out of the front door clutching my bag. I wrapped my woollen cape around me, covering my ever-tightening cotton shift dress and thin, worn, second-hand cardigan. My bare feet stayed cold inside my canvas pumps.

Safely away from the house I stopped and counted how much money I had left after giving Antonio my deposit of three pounds. Just enough for the bus fare to get to work and a pint of milk. At least my breakfast will be good for the baby, I thought as I stepped into the warmth of the corner shop.

'Shouldn't you be at school?' said the upright, busty lady, with a blue rinse, behind the counter. She was staring down at my bump with a hostile expression on her face.

'Just a pint of milk please,' I replied politely, fidgeting with my purse. I knew that I must have looked bedraggled and smelled like a vagrant, but there was nothing I could do about it.

By now workmen were coming into the shop to buy their Woodbines and Sun newspapers. I squeezed past to get out, embarrassed as they gloated over "girlie" magazines on the top shelf.

The icy pavements had not yet defrosted as I started to sip the milk. My hands were purple around the chilled bottle when suddenly it slipped to the ground. It smashed and filled the gutter with a smooth white river. Warm silent tears flowed down my cheeks to join it.

The bus arrived. As usual, the school kids laughed and joked about my bump but I was used to it. I felt I deserved their ridicule. I knew I looked much younger than my age, but they could not know how much I envied them…

'Come in my office,' shouted the manager. She beckoned me from across the room where we all sat around a large table sifting through public survey results, searching for statistics.

'Come in and sit down. My God you look so pale. Have you been up all night or what?' Without waiting for an answer she added, 'Here, get these down you. Two cod-liver oil capsules a day while you are working here.'

'But …'

'No buts, it's an order from your boss. Now go back out there to work.'

All eyes were on me, pretty amazed at what just happened. The Boss was known as the Rottweiler, yet her frown had softened as she spoke. She meant well and I was grateful. I forced a weak smile.

My coworkers gathered around me.

'What on earth has happened to you?' What's wrong?'

I told them what had gone on with Antonio. Kiki, a middle-aged woman from Puerto Rico, with long false nails and the ever-present smell of Chanel No 5, spoke in a harsh tone,

'Disgusting how some men seem to have a thing about pregnant women.'

What did I know about men? My experience was limited to boys. These women had been kind and empathic once they knew of my plight, often bringing me fruit or homemade flapjacks. They warned me about Mother and Baby Homes where the authorities were quick to take your baby away shortly after the birth to give to "deserving" childless couples who were queuing up. After visiting one of those homes, I was determined to keep my baby.

Those same ladies used to tease me when I opened my lunch bag every day to find Mrs Dean had made me thick-bread sandwiches with strong cheese and huge dollops of pickle. I'd told her I didn't like cheese or pickle. That was all she was prepared to make. They went in the bin every day and I believed that hunger was my punishment.

Christine, our team leader, appraised me with compassionate eyes.

'You're not going back there. You're coming home with me. We have a spare room, it's not big but you'll be safe. Anything you need picking up, my Pete can collect for you tomorrow.'

It was hard to accept such kindness. I was not used to it. I swallowed back the tears and thought, I never knew that good things could make your heart ache as much as the bad.

'Where's the father, if I may ask? He should be here with you,' said Chris as we clocked out and walked to her car.

Chris and Pete had not been married long. She was a big-built young woman with long jet-black hair and a curved nose. I couldn't understand why she had plucked out all her natural eyebrows and painted on high-raised black ones. She had a kind smile and I liked her. Chris told me that she would never be able to have children herself and I wondered what it must have been like to see me, a teenager, nearly eight months gone, with no home, no money, and no husband.

The little two-up, two-down brick cottage, with the bathroom off their bedroom, was their first home together. Stepping straight into the living room from the pavement, Chris pointed out the back room.

'If you feel down just go into that room and watch the tropical fish swimming around their tank, oblivious of our world. Somehow it can help all troubles go away.'

'That's what I do,' she added as she went on out to the kitchen to get the dinner on.

'Thank you, you're so good to me. Are you sure Pete won't mind me being here? I won't be any trouble, I swear. I just need to sort myself out.'

Pete was a taxi driver. He was shorter than Chris and fair-haired with tattoos on both arms. He had served some time in the army but had been discharged on medical grounds. With me pregnant, they both took to smoking their pot outside in the yard, which I thought was a kind gesture given that my bump and I were the intruders.

The next day, Pete went to the Italian's house, got my three pounds back and picked up the old cot and my carrier bag of possessions, which included a turquoise-and-white Babygrow embroidered with a little elephant. Antonio had the cheek to ask Pete for the other ten shillings I was supposed to give him at the end of the week. Pete was not to be messed with, so I asked no questions and was just truly grateful for what he had done for me.

The weekend arrived, by which time I knew every fish in the tank and had given each one a name. I liked that little back room. Chris came in and sat down.

'You never answered me when I asked where the father is. Do you hear from him? Does he know he will be a dad?'

I took my eyes off the fish and leaned back in the easy chair, hugging the blue velvet cushion.

'I've tried to stop thinking about him. We've lost touch over the past six months. Last I knew, he was in London and hanging out with other Chinese students.'

I stared back into the fish tank. A large angel fish was chasing some pretty little guppies.

'We met at an alternative boarding school, you know. We were both like fish out of water.

I fell silent. Chris smiled and touched my arm.

'Well, Pete and his pal will take you to find him. He really should be here with you now. You've not long to go. Write me a list of all the places he might be.'

It was a short list: Hong Kong House in Marylebone, Café des Artistes, a nightclub in Earls Court, and a Chinese restaurant where he helped out sometimes in South Kensington and, an address for one of his friends who lived in Warwick Avenue, near Paddington.

At six o'clock, Pete arrived from his day's work with his friend. After dinner, we set off in his Ford Cortina on the dark, wet roads to Warwick Avenue. I sat in the back and traced the raindrops with my finger as they slid down the cold windowpane making patterns. A sharp kick in my belly reminded me I was not alone.

The hypnotic squeak of the windscreen wipers was lulling me to sleep. Lyrics began playing in my head. *"Yesterday, all my troubles seemed so far away, now I need a place to hide away"*... There seemed comfort in Paul McCartney's voice. I sank back into the seat.

The jolt of the handbrake woke me. In the yellow glow of the streetlamp, I could see a three-storey house with a large black front door at the top of some steep steps. I stayed in the car while Pete and his pal got out and went up to knock on the door. A young Chinese man opened it. I couldn't hear what was said, but the man went back inside, and for a moment, I felt it had been a wasted journey. Then suddenly, there was Eddie, silhouetted in the doorway, looking small. He seemed as shocked to be found as I was to find him.

Later when I asked Pete what he'd said, he laughed. 'Simple. I told him he was about to be a father and he should get his stuff and come with us.'

It had been as easy as that. No arguing or putting up a fight. His family in Hong Kong had cut him off financially when he refused to continue his studies here. Perhaps he wanted to be rescued from where he had ended up living. Like me, he had one carrier bag of possessions.

The journey back to Pete and Chris's was a silent one. Me with my distended tummy and him with his now shoulder-length greasy hair and gaunt face. He looked at me and smiled – a smile that seemed to ask – *am I forgiven?*

I returned his smile, naively imagining all was going to be well and happy now we were together again. Two kids trying to play the game of life in a grown-up world we had arrived in much too soon.

Greenhouse Cocoon
by Juliet Coe

Glints of sunshine flash through the fluttering leaves of the gnarled apple tree, panes of glass beckoning me. I draw closer, see lights of the pond dance, bounce back from Grandpa's greenhouse out, into the garden, a twinkling oasis. Encompassing arms of the faded red brick wall frame this secluded space, absorbing and emitting heat as the sun's rays travel their well-worn orbit.

His back beginning to stoop, sparse hairs on shiny head, a chuckle never far away, Grandpa and I would retreat, he to garden, I to smell damp earth beds drying as the sun arced overhead; to brush fingers over the piles of terracotta pots; inhale the tender aroma of tomato leaves touched; pour cool water from the watering can and to press my hands against the rough brick wall that backed this glass house, absorb its heat and turn my head to the light.

I wonder, did he know when he tried to teach me of pruning, planting, songs of garden birds, when he left me to read in his space - did he know his eleven-year-old grandchild, far away from her Fijian home, breathed freely here, cocooned in the wall's warmth and shards of greenhouse light?

About The Memory Keepers

The Memory Keepers first met on an online memoir writing course in 2021 during Covid lockdown.

Micki Findlay has stories, articles and poetry published in several books and magazines, including Chicken Soup for the Soul, Crone Rising, Oasis Life, and Van Isle Poetry Collective. She writes her life stories to help other women recognise their self-worth, find hope through difficult circumstances, and realise they are not alone in their struggles. *www.mickifindlay.com*

Lindsay Tunstall studied Feature Writing and had two articles published in The Glasgow Herald. Writing in her capacity as a healthcare practitioner on health in the workplace, *Are You Sick at Work?* and *I Survived, So Many Others Will Not,* on the impact of malaria on the high death rate in The Gambia. She is the ghostwriter for a book on personal development and is currently working on a memoir of twenty years living in West Africa. *LindsayTunstallwriter@yahoo.com*

Suzi Bamblett has published three novels: *The Travelling Philanthropist, Three Faced Doll and Prescient Spirit. Imagined Dialogue* was featured on Daphne du Maurier's website. *The Girl on the Swing* was published by Shooter Literary magazine. *A Grandmother's Grief* was long-listed for the International Amy MacRae Award for Memoir. Other poems and short stories have appeared in Brighton University anthologies. Suzi graduated with a distinction for her MA in Creative Writing. *www.broodleroo.com*

Peta Heskell is a former coach, broadcaster and author of four personal development books in the *Flirt Coach* series, published by Thorsons Element. She has written for The Daily Mail, Psychologies, Cosmo, Permaculture News, Bride, Hypnotherapy Magazine and The Writer. Peta's memoir-in-progress covers her experiences living illegally in rural Georgia from 2008 to 2012 culminating in five months in two US jails. She features anecdotes about people and culture whilst exploring the decisions that upended her life. *www.facebook.com/sunnypetawriter*

Carol Prior is a choir leader, singer-songwriter, and performer who has written for the stage, most recently in her one-woman show *Give Me The Moonlight, Give Me The Girl* at The Beacon in Hastings. Her stories in this anthology are her first foray into memoir writing. *www.carolprior.com*

Stephanie Peart has published work online as part of her memoir writing course. The course programme prompted a writing journey exploring long-buried grief. She has written and performed her poetry at Headingley Literary Festival. As an adult educator, she ran creative writing sessions at community venues. She wrote her BA thesis, *Picturing Women*, on the invisibility of three women artists. *lysistrata21@gmail.com*

Sarah Lionheart is the author of *You Do Not Have to Be Good*, a memoir. Her poetry and literary reviews have appeared in Stanford Magazine. She has published articles on yoga, mindfulness and compassion in various magazines. Sarah has an MA in English from Stanford University and has taught creative writing to adults since 1984. *www.sarahlionheart.co.uk*

Delia Louise Seville has spent over two decades listening to other people's stories in her career as a psychotherapist. Now, she has embarked on telling her own story. *Bitter, Cold Days* is a short chapter from her memoir. *Cabins Apart* tells the story of an impulse acted on spontaneously in her fifties. *delialouisewriter@gmail.com*

Nicola Field is a published poet and author of the ground-breaking Marxist book on LGBTQ+ liberation, *Over the Rainbow*. She worked as a journalist and arts reviewer before beginning a PhD at Kingston University in the School of Art. Her research project weaves literary criticism, visual art and experimental creative writing to explore family trauma and neurodivergence. *www.nicolafield.co.uk*

Chassie Stone is a holistic beauty salon owner. She has published four articles in Professional Beauty and two short fiction stories in Woman's Own and Women's Weekly. Her article on spiritual perspectives appeared in The Inquirer, a Unitarian magazine. Chassie is working on two memoirs: *Keep the Wax Hot (How Not to Run a Beauty Business)* and *Empire Baby*. *chassieauthor1@gmail.com*

Juliet Coe is a former researcher and conference programme writer. Her first novel, *Bula Marama* (unpublished), was long-listed for the Blue Pencil Agency competition. She is currently working on a second novel. Juliet has poetic prose and flash fiction published in Rhyme & Reason and local anthologies. *Where Are You From?* was long-listed for the international Amy MacRae Award for Memoir. *julietcoe6@gmail.com*

Acknowledgements

Our gratitude to Alison Wearing and the Memoir Writing Ink team for your sensitive and insightful teaching and for encouraging us to tell our stories. Alison's course can be found at *www.memoirwritingink.com*.

We appreciate all you beta readers who saw our work in the early stages and provided valuable feedback.

A special mention to Carol Chambers for coming up with the idea of an anthology and seeing us through; Peta Heskell for the cover image, tech expertise and editing/proofreading; Lindsay Tunstall for proofreading/editing and Micki Findlay for marketing expertise and materials.